Titles in *The Bizarre Baron Inventions*

The Magnificent Flying Baron Estate

The Splendid Baron Submarine

The Wonderful Baron Doppelgänger Device

Praise for

The Magnificent Flying Baron Estate

"Kids will want to come along for this action-packed flight as Waldo defines his true character and learns how to be his best self."

—*Story Monsters Ink*

". . . about as wild as one might hope the West can get."

—*Kirkus Reviews*

"*The Magnificent Flying Baron Estate* is an enjoyable old-school Western with a contemporary feel . . . kids ages 9-12 are bound to enjoy this topsy-turvy tale with its funny moments of slapstick comedy."

—*The Children's Book Review*

"Readers who enjoyed the movie Up and "Wallace and Gromit" will embrace this humorous tale—all while learning about science, language, humanity, and family in the bargain."

—*School Library Journal*

THE BIZARRE BARON INVENTIONS

THE SPLENDID BARON
SUBMARINE

Eric Bower

Amberjack Publishing
New York, New York

Amberjack Publishing
228 Park Avenue S #89611
New York, NY 10003-1502
http://amberjackpublishing.com

Publisher's Cataloging-in-Publication data
Names: Bower, Eric, author.
Title: The Splendid baron submarine / Eric Bower.
Series: The Bizarre Baron Inventions
Description: New York, NY: Amberjack Publishing, 2017.
Identifiers: ISBN 978-1-944995-25-6 (Hardcover) | 978-1-944995-39-3 (ebook) | LCCN 2017937082
Subjects: LCC Adventure and adventurers--Juvenile fiction. | Inventions--Juvenile fiction. | Inventors--Juvenile fiction. | Ghosts--Juvenile fiction. | Pirates--Juvenile fiction. | Buried treasure--Juvenile fiction. | United States--History--19th century--Juvenile fiction. | Adventure fiction. | Fantasy fiction. | Science fiction. | BISAC JUVENILE FICTION / Steampunk | JUVENILE FICTION / Action & Adventure / General | Classification: PZ7.B6758 Sp 2017 | [Fic]--dc23

Cover Design & Illustrations: Agnieszka Grochalska

Printed in the United States of America.

For George and Doris Erk.

TABLE OF CONTENTS

Very Peculiar
Underwear, Stephen
September 14TH, 1891

"And that's when the killer monkeys showed up. They all started to attack me, slapping me senseless with their big monkey paws, when suddenly—"

"Thank you, Waldo," Miss Danielle said quickly. "That was a very . . . *interesting* report. But I think we've heard enough fiction for today."

I winced, just as I did every time someone called me Waldo instead of W.B., since W.B. is what I prefer to be called. But then I smiled and nodded my head, happy that my teacher had appreciated my report to the class about how I had spent my summer.

It wasn't until I had sat back down at my desk that I realized I might have misunderstood what she'd said.

"Wait, Miss Danielle?" I said, raising my hand. "Is fiction the one that is true, or the one that is made up?"

"Made up," Miss Danielle answered. "Fictional stories are made up, and nonfiction stories are true. Now, class, we will be discussing—"

"But it's not fiction," I interrupted her. "What I said was the absolute truth. And I can prove it."

I heard the rest of the students begin to whisper and giggle to their friends. They always whispered to their friends whenever I talked about my family. It used to bother me when they'd do that. In fact, sometimes I'd whisper along with them, so I wouldn't feel left out. I'd look around and whisper long words like "hasenpfeffer" and "sousaphone," so it would seem like I had friends in class too.

But now I've sort of gotten used to the whispers, as well as the names they call me, and the scorpions they hide in my lunch box, and the hot coals they slip into my trousers, and the kid who sits behind me who occasionally decides to give me a haircut without me asking for one. I suppose you can get used to just about anything if you deal with it for long enough.

Except maybe the hot coals. I'm still not too fond of them.

"You cannot prove a single word of your story," Miss Danielle told me as she went to the closet and pulled out a large, cone-shaped hat, "because it did not happen. It's obviously a lie, which you've made up in order to get attention. Now go sit in the corner and wear the dunce cap until you're ready to tell the truth."

"That pointy dunce cap sure looks a lot like the hats that were worn by the ghosts who were—"

"That's enough, Waldo Baron!" Miss Danielle interrupted, angrily stuffing my head into the dunce cap. "I won't listen to any more of your ridiculous stories. Go sit in the corner, right now."

The other children laughed. I walked to the corner and sat in what had become my regular seat in class, while wearing what had become my regular hat. I didn't really mind wearing the dunce cap. It kept my head warm, and it made me a good eighteen inches taller, too. Plus, it provided great protection for when I'd trip and land on my head, which you could say I did more than the average kid.

As I sat in the corner, I stared at the little hole in the wall and waited for Howard to come out.

I'd recently learned that a small family of mice lived in

the wall of the Pitchfork schoolhouse. At first I thought that it was just one mouse, which I named Howard. But there are actually five different mice in there, which I've also named Howard. The Howards like to poke their heads out and stare at me while I'm sitting in the corner, thinking about what I've done to upset Miss Danielle and the class.

I waved to the mousy face that poked out of the hole. Howard stared at me and shook its head. Howard can't believe that I'm in trouble yet again. I can't believe it either.

Believe it or not, I'm not actually a bad kid. I just have a lot of strange adventures with my parents, Sharon and McLaron Baron (I call them M and P, and they're quite possibly the cleverest inventors in the country), as well as their assistant, Rose Blackwood (whose brother, Benedict Blackwood, is quite possibly the worst criminal in the country), and my Aunt Dorcas (who is quite possibly the eggiest and weepiest aunt in the country). And sometimes, when I try to tell people about these strange adventures, they think I'm lying.

It's really not my fault. Miss Danielle is the one who

always asks us to give reports on what we do during our holiday breaks, and what our parents do for a living. I just tell her the truth, and then she puts the dunce cap on my head and makes me sit in the corner. I suppose I could lie and tell her I do all the boring things that the other kids do with their families, like shear sheep, sew bonnets, and plant potatoes, but I don't like to lie. I'm not particularly good at lying.

Are you confused?

Alright, let me give you an example. Here is the report I just gave to my class about how I spent my summer vacation . . .

There was a knock at the door.

"Oh dear," P said. "I wonder how we're supposed to answer that."

A knock on the door isn't usually a problem for us. But P had just shown us his newest invention, a nifty little device that he named the Gravity-Switcher-Ma-Thinger.

He wasn't the greatest at naming his inventions.

The Gravity-Switcher-Ma-Thinger looked a bit like a

glow-in-the-dark accordion, and when you pressed a button at the end of it, it caused the gravity in the room to flip. The force that normally pulled you to the floor would suddenly start pulling you up to the ceiling, which was why my parents and Rose Blackwood and I were all currently on the ceiling. In fact, everything in the living room was on the ceiling, including our sofa, chairs, table, lamps, the area rug, and our bookshelves.

This is the sort of thing that happens quite regularly here at the Baron Estate.

"W.B.!" M said angrily. "I told you to sweep the floors this morning. All of the dust and dirt from the floor is now up here. The ceiling is filthy!"

"Sorry."

My stomach was flipped upside down as well, and I was

finding it very difficult to keep down the bacon, cheese, pickle, tomato, fried onion, and jalapeno sandwich that I had eaten for my third breakfast. It was rather dizzying to be experiencing the living room upside down, and I can't say that I enjoyed it. I missed our normal gravity, which kept us all safely on the ground where we belonged.

"I think I prefer having the ceiling as the floor and the floor as the ceiling," P declared, resting his fists on his hips. "It just feels right. Perhaps I should make this a permanent change in the Baron Estate. From now on, we are an upside down family!"

P was the only one of us who actually looked like he was upside down, but that's because my father *always* looked like he was upside down, even when he was rightside-up. My father's hair is always standing straight up from the root. You see, his head is rather fond of lightning (he's been struck by lightning over twenty times), and every time it hits him, his white hair turns a shade whiter, and stands up in wild porcupine spikes.

And, believe it or not, that's not even one of the top ten weirdest things about my father.

"Um, Mr. and Mrs. Baron?" Rose said quickly. "I can tell from the look on W.B.'s face that he's about to be sick. That will be really gross and really difficult to clean from the ceiling later on."

"Oh dear," said M as she frowned at me. "He is a bit green, isn't he?"

I held in a burp.

There was another knock at the door, and this one sounded a bit more urgent. My father walked over to the wall and tried to grab the doorknob. But he couldn't reach it, even when he stood on his tiptoes. I've noticed that most doorknobs aren't located in a place on the door that allows people who are on the ceiling to reach them. That's clearly a silly design flaw, not to mention incredibly inconsiderate towards our country's upside down population . . . which I suppose just consisted of my family.

"Perhaps I should invent some sort of an arm extender," P said as he thoughtfully stroked his nose. "That way I wouldn't have so much trouble answering the door."

"Or you could just turn off the Gravity-Switcher-Ma-Thinger?" M suggested. "Whoever is at the door might be upset if they were to walk inside and suddenly fall up to the ceiling."

"That's true. Especially if W.B. gets sick all over it," P agreed. Then, without warning, he switched off the Gravity-Switcher-Ma-Thinger.

Everyone and everything fell from the ceiling to the

floor. No one was seriously hurt, though a bookshelf did land on my head. But my head had been through worse. My head attracts heavy things in the same way that P's head attracts lightning. I wish I had inherited M's head, which didn't really seem to attract much of anything.

With our living room now in shambles, M stood up and went to the door, adjusting her glasses and hair before opening it.

"Hello," she said. "How may I help you?"

Two of the largest men that I'd ever seen slowly lumbered into our home. They looked like a pair of gorillas that had been shaved and stuffed into suits, though that would be a pretty lousy thing to do to a gorilla.

One of the men was holding a piece of paper up to his face and reading from it very carefully. I could tell by the creases in his forehead that reading was not one of his favorite things to do. In fact, I could actually *hear* the sounds of his brain straining to understand the words, and it was not a pleasant noise. It sounded very squishy, like someone stepping on an old pumpkin.

"Mr. McLaron Baron?" he finally said to my mother, in a rather dopey sounding voice.

"No, but you're close," M told him politely. "I'm his wife. What can I do for you, sir?"

The large man looked back at his paper and struggled to read for a moment, his eyebrows bouncing like a pair of rabid caterpillars, before looking up again.

"Mrs. Sharon Baron?" he said.

"That's me."

The other large man pointed to me and Rose.

"And those two is Rose Blackwood and Waldo Baron?"

I winced. I really hate it when people call me Waldo. It's pretty high on my list of my least favorite things to be called, along with "weirdo," "chubby," "dummy," "clumsy," and "Julia," which is what the weird old man at the grocery store calls me.

"Yes, we *are*. And who might you be?" my mother asked the men, emphasizing the correct grammar.

"It don't matter who we are," one of the large men said gruffly. "We're gonna need you all to come with us."

"Yeah," the other one echoed. "We're gonna need you all to come with us."

"Alright," said my father, who stepped forward to follow them out the door, despite the fact that he wasn't wearing shoes.

My father is a genius, but sometimes he can be very scatterbrained and naive. I'd like to blame it on all the times that his head's been struck by lightning, but he's always been like that. He's just a unique person, which I suppose is a nice way of saying that he's a bit of a nut.

"Wait, McLaron," my mother said as she caught my father by the arm. "I don't think we should go anywhere with these men until they tell us who they are, as well as what they want, and where they're expecting us to go."

"I told you," one of the men grunted as he scratched the inside of his nose with his thumb. "It don't matter who we are."

"Yeah, it don't matter who we are," the other one echoed.

"Yeah, it don't matter who they are, Sharon," my father told my mother. "Let's go with them. You're always so suspicious of large and dangerous looking strangers who come to our door and give us mysterious orders. I don't understand why."

As you can see, it's not particularly difficult to convince my father to do something. Usually all you have to do is repeat yourself a few times. Luckily, my mother has much better sense than my father, or we'd all be in a lot of trouble.

"What happens if we refuse to go with you?" my mother asked the men.

The two men began to pound their fists into their

palms.

"Oh, you'll be going with us," said one of them. "We guarantee it."

"Yeah, we guarantee it," the other echoed.

"Why do you always repeat what the other guy says?" I asked. "Do you think we're not hearing him?"

The echoing man blushed, but then he pounded his palm with his fist even harder.

"You're coming with us, or we're going to play the song 'Camptown Races' on your spines," he growled, and then whistled the first few notes from "Camptown Races."

"Camptown Races" was a catchy tune that we'd been singing around the Baron Estate for the past few weeks. It was currently our favorite song, and whenever one of us started to sing it, the others had to join in. We sang it at breakfast, lunch, and dinner; we sang it when we did our chores; and we sang it before we went to sleep at night. So when the large man whistled the opening notes to the song, I couldn't help but hum along. Rose Blackwood snapped her fingers, M tapped her feet, and P pulled two spoons from his pocket and began to slap them rhythmically against his thigh. Soon we were all tapping and humming, clapping and snapping, singing and whistling, while the two shaved gorillas began to whoop and twirl as we had ourselves a little "Camptown Races" hoedown. One of the men showed us a new dance called "the stinky onion," which was a lot of fun to do until I somehow managed to get my head stuck in the fireplace.

The fun always stops when my head gets stuck in the fireplace.

"While I do love 'Camptown Races,' I'm sorry to say that it's not possible for you to play that song on our spines," my father told the two large men when we had all finished dancing. "You see, a spinal column wouldn't produce the proper variety of notes due to its shape. Now, if you were to take our rib cages, you might be able to play them like a xylophone if you—"

One of the men grabbed my father's lips and pinched them tightly together so he couldn't speak. They clearly weren't interested in learning which parts of our bodies they could use as musical instruments.

"You talk too much," the man told him.

"Mmmmphllegnnnmm," P agreed through his smushed lips.

The men then began to pull my father towards the door by his mouth.

"Stop that!" M cried.

"Let go of him!" warned Rose Blackwood. "Or else."

"Or else *what*?" asked the man pulling my father's face.

"Yeah, or else what?" the other one echoed, then he blushed as he glanced at me.

"Yhhmomehmhuhhff?" my father asked.

"Or else . . ." Rose began, and then looked to me for help.

Back when she was still trying to be a villain (like her evil brother), Rose Blackwood carried a gun. But she didn't carry one anymore. Now she was an inventor's assistant, which was a much more respectable job, though it meant she only carried inventor things, like small tools, and pencils, and rulers, and goggle cleaner, and throat spray for when my parents' throats hurt from too much maniacal inventor laughter.

Suddenly I had an idea. I don't get them often, but when I do get them, they tend to be doozies.

"Or else this!" I cried, grabbing the Gravity-Switcher-Ma-Thinger and pressing the button on the end.

Suddenly, everything and everyone on the floor was once again on the ceiling, including the two shaved gorillas.

"Oh dear, I forgot to tell them to wipe their feet," M said with a sigh. "Now there will be scuff marks all over the ceiling."

The two men were unable to wipe their feet, since

they'd both been knocked unconscious by the confusing fall up to the ceiling. They hadn't expected to fall up because no one ever expects to fall up. It would be like expecting a tap dancing duck to suddenly pop out of your birthday cake. You can hope for it, but it probably isn't going to happen.

Probably.

Rose took the paper that one of the men had been holding and quickly read it.

"Good thinking, W.B.," my father said to me. "I was beginning to miss the ceiling as well. It's much nicer up here."

"That's not why he did it, dear," M said, patting P on his spiky head. "And that was a very clever way of saving us, W.B., though I'm still upset with you for not sweeping the floor."

"Sorry."

"Mr. and Mrs. Baron?" Rose said. "You should take a look at this."

"What is it, Rose?" M asked.

Rose handed the paper to my mother, who adjusted her glasses and read from it out loud.

"Mongo and Knuckles, please collect Mr. McLaron Baron, Mrs. Sharon Baron, Waldo Baron, and Rose Blackwood from the Baron Estate, and bring them to me. Do not tell them your names, and do not answer any of their questions. Sincerely, Levi P. Morton V.P.U.S."

"V.P.U.S? What does V.P.U.S. stand for?" I asked.

"I'm pretty sure it stands for 'Very Peculiar Underwear, Stephen,'" my father answered.

"V.P.U.S. stands for 'Vice President of the United States,'" my mother told me.

"Are you sure?"

She nodded knowingly.

"I'm positive. Levi P. Morton is the name of the current Vice President of the United States, so this letter must have been written by him. What else could V.P.U.S. stand for?"

I looked at my father, who shrugged his shoulders and once again mouthed:

"Very Peculiar Underwear, Stephen."

HAS SOMEONE BEEN EATING MY DECORATIVE ROCKS?

When Mongo and Knuckles finally woke up, we agreed to go along with them. We were dying to know what the Vice President of the United States could want with us. And we were also quite curious why he would choose to send two hairy-knuckled goons like Mongo and Knuckles to find us. Surely, the Vice President of the United States could have sent some of his more respectable employees to our home, but, then again, we didn't know a whole lot about politics. Maybe politicians just preferred to work with goons. Goons were quite good at gooning, and sometimes you just needed a good gooning goon in order to get some good goonery done.

"You need to stop making up stupid words," Rose told

me when I explained that to her.

We decided to trick Mongo and Knuckles (who seemed as though they had brains the size of red bopple nuts) into giving us some information about our secret invitation to see the Vice President.

"We've decided to go along with you without asking any questions," M told them.

"Good," said Knuckles. "Because we wouldn't have answered any."

"Well, we wouldn't want you to," I retorted.

"Yes, you would," said Mongo. "If you knew what this was about, you'd want to ask us at least one hundred and seven different questions. Maybe even one hundred and eight."

"I doubt that," Rose said. "I bet it's something really boring."

"Yes, you probably just want us to come over and give you gardening tips," my mother added.

"You couldn't be more wrong," said Knuckles.

"I actually wouldn't mind some gardening tips," Mongo said hopefully. "My tomato plants keep dying before they sprout. What am I doing wrong? Should I use fertilizer? What *is* fertilizer? Someone told me that it's just cow plop, but I think they was funnin' me."

"Be quiet, Mongo," Knuckles told him.

"You weren't supposed to let them know our names, Knuckles," Mongo pointed out.

"Then why did you just say *my* name, Mongo?" Knuckles asked through gritted teeth.

I yawned as loudly as I could, as we walked outside and stepped into the large horse drawn carriage parked in front of our white picket fence. Once we were inside the carriage, Mongo and Knuckles tied blindfolds over our eyes.

"This is going to be the dullest afternoon ever," I said as they finished tying my blindfold.

"No, it ain't," said Mongo. "It's going to be exciting."

"It'll be about as exciting as watching paint dry."

"This is ten times more exciting than that! Maybe even more! Don't make me do the math!"

"Excuse me while I take a nap," I said. "Wake me up when we get to Dullsville, which is obviously where we're headed. Dull, dull, dull . . ."

"There ain't nothing dull about meeting the Vice President!" Mongo snapped.

Knuckles knuckled Mongo over the head.

"You weren't supposed to tell them about the Vice President!" Knuckles screamed. "Remember, you blockhead? He told us not to mention that, or the part about him needing the Barons to invent something for him."

Mongo mongoed Knuckles over the head.

"You weren't supposed to say that he needs them to invent something for him!" Mongo shouted. "Vice President Morton told us that after he told us about the island!"

"YOU WEREN'T SUPPOSED TO MENTION THE ISLAND!" Knuckles roared. "YOU'VE RUINED EVERYTHING!"

And, because goons can only scream at each other for so long before their fists become antsy and anxious to join the disagreement, Mongo and Knuckles began to fight one another. They punched each another with powerful hands the size of honey-baked hams, though nowhere near as tasty. Even though my parents hate it when people fight, they were smart enough not to get between the two men, who, as I mentioned before, really did seem more like gorillas than humans, both in appearance and in smell.

By the time the carriage had reached its destination, Mongo and Knuckles had beaten each other black and blue, and a little bit orange as well. They grumbled at one another as they led us out of the carriage and took off our blindfolds.

We found ourselves standing in front of a large, white building with several sets of tall columns in front of it. It was a very official-looking building, like the sort of building you'd be embarrassed to set foot in if you'd forgotten to change your underwear that day (wait a minute . . . did I remember to . . . oh, bother). It didn't look like any of the other houses that I'd seen in Arizona Territory. For one thing, it was pretty clean. The houses in our area were usually so covered with dirt and desert dust that you couldn't tell what color they'd originally been painted.

I looked around and wondered where we were. It appeared we were in the middle of a desert, though I had no idea which desert. There were no other buildings or houses to be seen, no signs or roads. This building seemed like a pretty good place for an important person to stay if he didn't want to be bothered by anyone.

There was a pair of very serious-looking men dressed in long, black coats who were standing in front of the building. They looked as though they were guarding it. They slowly opened the front doors as they nodded their heads at us and pointed inside.

Mongo and Knuckles limped ahead, leading us into a very tidy lobby, then down a long and winding hallway. The hallway was dark and narrow, and there were pictures on the wall that had been flipped over so we couldn't see what was on them. They must have been top secret, though

I wasn't sure what a top secret picture might be. Perhaps they were pictures of aliens. Or secret weapons. Or secret alien weapons. Or maybe the owner of the building had a funny looking grandma they were secretly ashamed of. Who knows?

At the end of the hallway was a door with an American flag tacked to it. We all saluted the flag when we saw it, and then Knuckles knocked on the door.

"What's the password?" a funny sounding voice asked from inside.

"Weasel face," Knuckles answered.

There was the clicking sound of a heavy lock unlocking, and then the door slowly swung open, revealing a strange little man whose face was really quite weasely-looking. It was pointy in all the places where faces were usually smooth, and it was smooth in all the places where faces were usually pointy. And the places that were usually neither smooth nor pointy were just plain odd. He wore a dark suit, dark shirt, and a purple tie. His black hair was slicked back over his scalp with shiny hair wax.

"These are the Barons?" Weasel Face asked Knuckles and Mongo.

Weasel Face had a strong accent that sounded sort of like a cross between German, Chinese, Scottish, and the weird way your voice sounds when you can't breathe through your nose.

Knuckles and Mongo nodded.

"Well, sorta," said Mongo. "The pretty lady with black hair is named Rose Blackwood."

"And the short, fat, clumsy kid with the bad haircut says his name's W.B.," Knuckles added.

I glared at him to show that I was annoyed by his description of me.

I'm not short.

"Fine, fine. You two stand guard at the door," Weasel Face said to Mongo and Knuckles. "Come in, Barons, but please take off your shoes. We just had the floors cleaned."

My mother, Rose, and I took off our shoes and placed them on the shoe rack that Weasel Face pointed out to us. P tried to take his shoes off, but then he realized he'd forgotten to put them on back at the Baron Estate.

"What should I do?" he asked.

The weasel-faced man frowned as he looked at P's shoeless feet.

"I suppose you should take off your socks," he said. "Now come inside. We can't waste any more time."

P took off his socks and hung them neatly on the sock rack located beside the shoe rack. Weasel Face ushered us into a dimly lit office with wood paneled walls. There was a window at the other end of the office, but it was covered by a thick curtain. Next to the window was a huge bookcase filled with about a hundred different leather-bound books.

Weasel Face told us to sit down, so we all sat together on a long sofa which was positioned across from the biggest desk I'd ever seen. The desk had a kerosene lantern on it, which provided all of the light in the room. Behind the desk was a high-backed leather chair that was turned away from us.

It was a very important-looking office, the sort of office that a kid like me doesn't usually feel too comfortable in because we're usually screamed at any time we set foot in it. I sat with my hands in my lap and my knees pressed together, trying to breathe as quietly as possible so my unimportant breaths wouldn't bother the important office's owner.

"Are they all here, Veezlefayce?" a voice from behind the chair asked.

"Yes, sir," said Weasel Face with a weasely-faced frown. "They are."

"Wait, your actual name is Weasel Face?" I asked.

Rose coughed into her fist, trying to hide her laughter.

The foreign man looked as though he might explode.

"Not Weasel Face!" he hissed at me. "*Veezle*fayce! It is a very common last name in my country! Why does everyone here in the United States get it wrong? It's Veezlefayce! *Veezlefayce!*"

"What does *Veezlefayce* mean in your language?" M asked.

"It means 'weasel face,' doesn't it?" Rose said with a grin.

"Of course it doesn't mean weasel face!" Veezlefayce snarled. "That would be ridiculous. It means 'kidney bean.'"

"That's enough, Veezlefayce," said the voice from behind the chair. "Please leave the room and let me speak with the Baron family alone. Make sure no one interrupts us."

Veezlefayce shot each of us a very ugly and weasely look before leaving the room. When he was gone, my father spoke.

"Mr. Vice President, it really is an honor to meet you, a wonderful honor, and we're very excited about it. I didn't vote for you, but you shouldn't feel bad about that. And frankly, neither should I. After all, you didn't vote for me either."

The chair suddenly spun around, revealing a very surprised-looking Vice President Levi P. Morton. He was a short man with a huge mustache, and he was dressed in an uncomfortable-looking suit. He looked like a very important man, and a bit like a turtle as well. A very important turtle.

"How did you know it was me?" he demanded from beneath his huge mustache. "Was it Veezlefayce? Did he tell you? If so, I'll need to have a very unpleasant conversation with that weasel-faced fool . . ."

"No, he didn't tell us," M said quickly. "It was just a lucky guess, sir. I suppose your office just looks like the office of a vice president, that's all. What can we do for you?"

"You need an invention?" Rose asked.

"Something about an island?" I added.

Levi P. Morton looked at us as though we'd just slapped him across the face with a wet trout. He was utterly shocked at how much we seemed to know.

"Were those lucky guesses too?" he asked.

My family and Rose exchanged a glance. We do that a lot, especially when we're lying about something.

"Yes," said M. "Yes, they were."

"Well," Vice President Morton grumbled, "I suppose you are quite clever. All of that is true. I am the Vice President, and this is my private West Coast office, and I do need your help. I read about you transforming your home into some sort of a flying machine. That's truly brilliant. In fact, it's quite possibly the most brilliant invention I've ever heard of."

"Aw, shucks," said P as he shined his knuckles on his vest. "You're just saying that because it's true."

"I've also heard about several other adventures that you've had, and other clever inventions you've invented," the Vice President continued. "And it's because of your cleverness, as well as your talent for unique inventions, that I'd like to make you a very strange and very specific offer."

"How strange?" I asked.

"How specific?" P asked.

"What's the offer?" asked M.

The Vice President stood up and cleared his throat. He started to pace back and forth.

"The funny thing about money," he began, "is that people always say *it doesn't grow on trees*, despite the fact that money is made of paper, and paper comes from trees. This has always confused me. But that's not the point. The point is that this country has run out of money. It's our own fault. Our government has been spending money on all sorts of ridiculous things, like solid gold mustache combs, diamond studded toilet seats, edible windows, waterproof wigs, and that giant copper statue we bought from France. Now we're completely broke. I warned them about wasting money on that statue. And also about the toilet seats . . ."

I noticed a candy dish on the Vice President's desk.

"I see," said P, as he took out his wallet. "And now you'd like to borrow some money. Alright. How much do you need?"

"I don't think he's asking us for money, Mr. Baron," Rose told my father.

"She's right," Vice President Morton said. "The amount of money that we need is far greater than you'd be able to fit into your wallet. We recently borrowed one million dollars from another country, and if we are unable to pay them back, it will make our country look bad. How bad, you ask? Very, very bad. Will it make our country a laughingstock? Yes, it might. Will we recover from it? I don't know. Will the rest of the world stop trusting us? Possibly. Do I like to ask myself questions and then answer them? No. I don't like that."

There were jelly beans in the candy dish.

I *love* jelly beans.

"Well, I can understand why the country that our government borrowed money from would be angry with us,"

M said to the Vice President. "After all, you should always pay people back when you borrow from them. It's the right thing to do."

"But we can't pay them back!" Levi Morton cried. "Don't you see? We don't have one million dollars to give to them! Money doesn't grow on trees! Even though it's made from trees! Which is very confusing! But that's not the point! The point is, there is an island in the South Pacific, a very beautiful little island without a name."

I wanted those jelly beans very badly.

"I see," said my father. "And you would like us to name the island for you."

"No," said Vice President Morton. "There is a sunken treasure in the waters surrounding that island. And I want you to find it."

He turned around and grabbed an old book from his bookshelf.

When he did, I quickly leaned forward and grabbed a handful of jelly beans from his candy dish.

The Vice President opened the book to a specific page that he had marked and then dropped it on the desk for us to see. There was an illustration of a tropical island, and on the shore of the island was a pirate with a treasure chest. I could tell that he was a pirate because he had a pirate hat on his head, an eyepatch over one eye, a hook where his right hand should be, a peg where his left leg should be, a tattoo on his chest, earrings in both his ears, a scar on his neck, a bottle of rum in his hand, his beard was blue, his timbers were shivered, he had a parrot on each shoulder, and he wore a little sash that said PIE-RAT on it.

"This is Captain Affect the Pirate. You might have heard of him. He is the richest and most successful pirate thief of all time. Actually, there might have been more successful pirate thieves before him, but Captain Affect made certain to steal all of the history books that mentioned them. His favorite ship reportedly sank somewhere around this island, taking his greatest and most impressive treasure to the bottom of the sea. I need you to invent something that can find that sunken treasure, which is hidden somewhere in the dark surrounding waters. If you can find the treasure for us, then our country can pay back all of the money that it owes. Do you understand?"

"Of course we understand, but what's in it for us?" Rose asked carefully. "This sounds like it's going to be a very difficult task which will take quite a bit of time, energy, and resources. Are you going to pay us for finding Captain Affect's treasure?"

The Vice President smiled, slowly turning the page in

his book.

As he did, I quickly stuffed the handful of jelly beans into my mouth.

The next page in the book showed a drawing of the largest diamond I had ever seen. It was absolutely stunning, shining and shimmering like the brightest star in the night sky, perfectly cut and projecting a gorgeous glow. It was so beautiful that I had a hard time believing it was real.

The jelly beans were a bit stale.

"This," Vice President Morton whispered as he pointed to the picture, "is the Wish Diamond. You might have heard of this as well. This diamond was the crown jewel of Captain Affect's loot, and it is famous for being the most beautiful and *most stolen* diamond in history. Captain Affect stole it from a king, who had stolen it from a prince, who had stolen it from a sheik, who had stolen it from a princess, who had stolen it from a sultan, who had stolen it from a duke, who had stolen it from a queen, who had stolen it from an emperor, who had stolen it from a guy named Greg."

The jelly beans were actually very stale. I choked as I tried to chew them.

"It's very beautiful," said a wide-eyed M.

"It's incredibly lovely," agreed an equally wide-eyed P.

"It's yours," said Vice President Morton. "And I mean the actual diamond, not just this picture of the diamond. All you need to do is find the rest of the treasure, and I'll let you keep the greatest diamond in history as a reward. What do you say, Barons? Will you agree to go on this treasure hunt in order to save your country from shame?"

"I agree," P said proudly, with diamonds shimmering in his eyes.

"I agree," M said, with a diamond inspired grin.

"I agree," said Rose Blackwood, whose fingers traced the picture of the Wish Diamond in the book.

"GLURK!" I said.

Vice President Morton frowned at me.

"Glurk?" he repeated.

"Is that an agreeing GLURK or a disagreeing GLURK, W.B.?" P asked.

"W.B., dear, why is your face turning blue?"

"GLURK!"

Vice President Morton looked down at his candy dish.

"Goodness," he said. "Has someone been eating my decorative rocks?"

I Thought It Was
a Hairy Baby

After Rose had whacked me on the back hard enough to get me to spit up some of the decorative rocks I'd swallowed, Vice President Levi P. Morton made us swear that we wouldn't tell anyone about our secret treasure hunt. He didn't want the world to know that the Vice President of the United States was trying to raise money for the country by searching for a pirate thief's sunken loot.

"Here is a map to the island," he said, handing P a rolled up piece of parchment paper. "And, please, Barons, be very careful. There are all sorts of dangerous animals in the surrounding waters, like sharks and electric eels and rockfish and swordfish and possibly even gunfish. There are also rumors that the entire area is haunted by Captain

Affect's pirate curse. So be on the lookout for *ghosts*."

I couldn't help but smirk. A pirate curse? Ghosts? Really? The Vice President of the United States *actually* believed in *ghosts?* That sounded sillier to me than a claustrophobic gopher. I looked to my parents to see how they'd respond.

"I don't believe in ghosts," M told the Vice President. "In fact, none of us do."

"Good, yes, very good," said Vice President Morton with an enthusiastic nod. "And when you see the ghosts, be sure to tell them that. It'll confuse them."

We all shook hands, and, after I had promised to replace the Vice President's decorative rocks that I'd swallowed, we quickly left his office and bumped into a very annoyed-looking Veezlefayce.

Actually, I can't really say for certain if he was annoyed or not. I was sort of getting the impression that his face just looked that way. I'll bet he was annoyed looking even as a weasel-faced baby.

"I will lead you out, Barons," he told us with an annoyed looking smile. "And do not tell anyone about this meeting. Tell no one! Once you have found the treasure and returned home, we will meet you at the Baron Estate and collect the treasure from you. That means that you are not to come back here. Do not come back here! Have a lovely day. A lovely day!"

Mongo and Knuckles were waiting for us outside with our blindfolds, which they slipped over our heads one at a time. Once we were back in the carriage, my parents and Rose began to excitedly discuss possible inventions and ideas that could be used to find Captain Affect's sunken treasure.

"What about the Super-Grabber Device that you invented last week, Mrs. Baron?" Rose suggested. "We could sail a ship to the island and use the Super-Grabber to search for the treasure, and then pull it from the sea."

"I don't know about that," M said doubtfully. "How would we be able to see what we're searching for? We would need to attach some sort of super powered lantern to the Super-Grabber Device. Plus, the Super-Grabber Device isn't waterproof, and I don't think it's strong enough to pull a treasure chest out of the water. Hmmmm . . ."

"Oh! What if we used the Big Magnet to find the treasure?" Rose suggested.

"We can't use the Big Magnet; gold isn't magnetic," M told her. "Besides, we got rid of the Big Magnet because it was *way* too powerful, remember? The last time you used the Big Magnet, it caused that huge earthquake in Japan."

"We weren't going to mention that again," P said quietly. "There are still a lot of angry Japanese people who are asking questions . . ."

"Oh, that's right," M said as she nodded.

"Yes, let's keep thinking."

"Hmmm . . ." they all hmmmed together as they thought.

I hmmmed too, even though I wasn't trying to come up with a way to find the treasure. I didn't see the point in trying. After all, I had the least scientific brain out of all of them. Why should I even bother attempting to think of an idea? My parents were geniuses, and Rose Blackwood had already learned a lot from them by being their assistant. I knew nothing, other than the best way to deep fry a slice of pie. I was about as scientific as a turnip.

"We could catch a shark and train it to search for treasure," P said. "I mean, if you can train a dog to roll over and play dead, then why can't you train a shark to hunt for treasure?"

My father loves animals, and is always looking for any excuse to have a new pet, no matter how odd or dangerous that pet might be. If we ended up catching a shark and training it to search for treasure, then there was a very good chance it would end up living in our bathtub at the Baron Estate.

M and Rose politely suggested that they continue trying to think of another idea.

"Hmmmmm . . ." they all hmmmmmed.

"They sound like bees," Mongo whispered to Knuckles.

"Bees make honey," Knuckles whispered back knowingly.

Maybe it was because I was wearing a blindfold and had nothing to look at to distract me, or maybe it was because the long carriage ride was bumpy and had jolted my brain in a funny way, or maybe it's because I had almost died choking on fake jelly beans, but something weird happened in my mind that doesn't normally happen.

I had a *sort of* scientific idea.

Sort of.

"What about your little underwater ship?" I asked P. "You invented a little underwater ship at the same time that you invented the little winged flying machine that we flew around the world after we shrunk ourselves, remember? Why don't we use the underwater ship to search for the sunken treasure?"

"The underwater ship?" my mother repeated. "But that ship is so tiny, W.B. It's a miniature. We couldn't fit into that unless we shrunk ourselves to the size of squirrels again. And it would be too dangerous to travel under the sea in a ship that small. We'd likely be swallowed by a hungry fish."

"Right," I said. "But what if we made the little underwater ship *bigger?*"

"Bigger?" my father asked, suddenly sounding quite intrigued.

"Yes. Bigger. You already invented something that shrinks people to the size of squirrels and then returns them to their normal size. Couldn't you invent a machine that would simply make something bigger than usual? Something that could transform a little toy ship into a *real* ship? A *Bigging* Machine?"

For a moment no one spoke. I could tell they were all thinking about my suggestion and how they could shoot it down as a bad idea. They rarely used my ideas, but that's only because they were usually so terrible. But this one was different. I don't know if it was a particularly good suggestion, but it was definitely different.

"You know," my mother finally said, "that's a really interesting idea. A *Bigging Machine* to make things bigger. We could travel to the coast carrying the little underwater ship with us in our luggage. And then, once we've reached the sea, we can use the Bigging Machine to make the underwater ship bigger, and then use that to explore the waters surrounding the island! W.B., you're a genius!"

I burped up a decorative rock.

"Wait a minute," Rose Blackwood said. "I think we're getting ahead of ourselves. Is that even possible? Can you invent something like that, Mr. Baron?"

"Hmmm?" my father said. "Oh, I already did. I had some spare parts in my vest pockets, so after W.B. suggested the Bigging Machine, I quickly invented it. If my calculations are correct, it should work without a problem."

"Are you serious?" asked Mongo, sounding more dumbfounded than usual. "You invented a Bigging Machine with your eyes blindfolded? That sounds impossible."

"Hey, are you still wearing your blindfold?" Knuckles demanded.

"Can't you tell?" Rose asked.

For a moment, neither of the big men spoke.

I burped up another decorative rock.

"Wait a minute," M said to the goons. "Are you two wearing blindfolds as well?"

"... Maybe."

"Then how do you know we aren't peeking?" Rose asked. "Shouldn't you be keeping an eye on us to make sure we keep our blindfolds on?"

I heard a quick rustling noise, which sounded very much like two large gorillas quickly pulling off their blindfolds.

"Of course we ain't wearing blindfolds," Knuckles said

indignantly. "What do you think we is, stupid or something?"

We thought it would be best not to answer him.

The carriage arrived at the Baron Estate shortly after that, and my family and Rose quickly climbed out. Mongo and Knuckles waved goodbye to us with their blindfolds, before their carriage carried them away.

"Let's test it," M said.

"Test what?" P asked.

I burped up yet another mouthful of decorative rocks.

Sheesh, how many of those things did I swallow?

"The Bigging Machine," Rose said impatiently. "We should make sure it works before we try it on the underwater ship."

"Ah yes," P said, as he began to look around our large property. "What should I test it on first? Hmmmm, decisions, decisions . . ."

"How about that fence?" I suggested, pointing to the white picket fence that lined our yard.

P took his Bigging Machine, which looked a bit like a mechanical toothbrush for fish, and pointed it at the fence. He flipped a switch, and a bright blue light shot out of the end of the machine.

"Oops."

We all screamed.

The Bigging Machine worked perfectly.

However, there was a bit of a problem with my father's aim. He's a lousy shot. In fact, he's quite possibly the lousiest shot in the world. There's a reason why my mother refused to let him carry a pistol, or a rifle, or a bow and arrow set, and why he wasn't allowed to throw peanuts into the air so that he could try to catch them in his mouth (the last time he did that, he ended up in the hospital for six weeks, and almost had his left ear amputated). M said that P once tried to shoot a tin can off a fence post with a sling shot, and he ended up shooting himself in the back of the head. Twice.

When P fired the Bigging Machine, he missed the fence entirely, and instead he hit a bug. The bug then grew to the size of a small building. And it was not happy about that.

After the giant bug chased us around the Baron Estate

for about an hour, Rose finally had the idea to sneak into the work garage and find my father's Shrinking Invention. She pointed the Shrinking Invention at the bug and shrunk it back to its normal size. Then, we chased the bug around the yard for close to an hour, just to show it what it felt like. Once we had finished showing the bug what it felt like to be a bug, we decided to go inside.

P opened the front door and walked into the house. He immediately fell up to the ceiling.

The Gravity-Switcher-Ma-Thinger had been turned on again. There was only one person in the house who could have done that, and it had most likely been a terrible accident. That person was the only person living in the Baron Estate who had less interest in science and inventions than me. She was a person who was constantly upset by everything, a person who screamed at the drop of a hat (I'm dead serious—do not drop your hat in front of her), a person who was a world champion weeper . . .

"Finally!" cried a plum-faced Aunt Dorcas. "Help me! I've been stuck up here for the past six hours, and I really need to use the bathroom!"

While P and M went to their garage to study the map that the Vice President had given them, Rose and I cleaned up the mess in the living room. Aunt Dorcas went to her bedroom to sit up. She wanted to lie down, but all of the blood in her body had rushed to her head from crying and screaming on the ceiling for over six hours. It had turned her head bright purple. Aunt Dorcas was a very eggy looking woman, and having a purple head didn't really suit her. It probably wouldn't suit most people, come to think of it, unless of course your hair happened to be a fetching shade of blue.

"Isn't this exciting, W.B.?" Rose said to me as she swept. "A real life treasure hunt! And for the Vice President of the United States, too! We can actually save the country with our inventions."

"Yes. Ow!" I responded.

I said "yes" because I agreed that it was exciting. I said "ow" because I tripped over my shoelaces and landed on my face.

I should mention again that I actually am the clumsiest kid in the country. It's true. I expect to be given an award for it someday, a fancy trophy with a kid slipping on a banana peel at the top.

"Be careful, kiddo," Rose said to me with a smile.

"It's very exciting," I told her. "I've read about underwater ships in some of my adventure novels. They're called 'submarines.' The people who travel in them are able to see all sorts of amazing things under the sea. It's a whole different world down there, a world that we know very little about. It's going to be an amazing adventure."

Rose and I put up both of the bookcases, which, surprisingly enough, weren't too damaged after dropping from the ceiling three times. There was a dent in one of them, but that wasn't from the floor; it was from when it landed on my head. M often tells me I have the hardest and strongest skull she's ever seen. I'll probably be given an award for that after my award for clumsiest kid. It'll be a trophy with a kid on top who has a cannonball for a head.

"It's an exciting adventure," Rose Blackwood continued, "but at the same time, I have to admit that I'm a little nervous about it."

"I'm not nervous. I'm just excited."

"You're really not nervous at all?" she asked. "Really? Doesn't it seem rather dangerous to you, being trapped in that little metal ship underwater? What if it springs a leak? Or what if we run out of oxygen? Or what if we're attacked by a large sea creature, like a giant squid, or a giant eel, or a giant shark, or a giant cod? We'd be helpless."

None of those thoughts had occurred to me. Suddenly, I wished that my mind hadn't come up with the idea of a Bigging Machine. That's why I preferred not to think.

Thinking always seemed to get me into trouble.

You know what creature never really thinks or comes up with scientific ideas? A slug.

Have you ever heard of a slug getting itself into trouble with a scientific idea?

Of course you haven't.

"Okay, now I'm nervous. I don't want to go anymore. Why do people actually listen to my stupid ideas? What's wrong with all of you? How can we get out of going?"

Rose laughed, tousling my hair. "We can't. You heard Vice President Morton. Our country needs us to be heroes. We have to be brave."

I looked down at the medal I had pinned to my vest. That medal was given to me by Sheriff Hoyt Graham, a man who I used to idolize. According to the many books that had been written about him, Sheriff Graham was a fearless hero who fought off countless dangerous villains. In real life, however, he was a coward who had trouble fending off skunks. He gave me the medal after he told me that I was *his* hero for helping to capture Benedict Blackwood, the worst criminal in the country. The medal said "WORLD'S GREATEST GRANDMA."

Sheriff Graham had never learned to read.

But even though I wasn't a grandma (and even if I was,

I probably wouldn't be the world's greatest), I still took a lot of pride in that medal. I looked at it when I needed to be reminded that I could be heroic and brave.

We went to our rooms to pack our suitcases for the trip to the island. I wasn't sure what to bring, so I packed all of my clothes and underclothes, my shoes, my toothbrush, my pillow and blanket, my kerosene lantern, a comb, a pencil and a pad of paper, six of my books, three wheels of cheese, four loaves of bread, eighteen bars of chocolate, nineteen pieces of taffy, twenty chocolate chip cookies, nine apple tarts, and a blackberry pie I'd baked the day before.

Rose came into my room and showed me what she'd packed for the trip: a single change of clothes, her bathing suit, her bathing cap, and her toothbrush. All of her things fit neatly into one little handbag. I could barely fit all of my things into a big steamer trunk. I was pretty sure that I had crushed the blackberry pie, and that my socks and under-wear would now be soggy and delicious, but it was too late to repack everything. Plus I didn't want to.

"That's all you're bringing?" I asked her. "We might be

gone for weeks."

She thought about that for a moment.

"You're right. I might need a second bathing suit."

We brought our luggage downstairs and placed it alongside M and P's trunks and suitcases. P used his Shrinking Invention to shrink our luggage, which made it much easier to carry. We placed our luggage into the palms of our hands and walked outside.

"How are we getting to the shore?" I asked.

P pulled out the little winged flying machine that we had used to fly around the world several months earlier. P and M had called it an "Air Oh! Plane", because you used it to fly through the "air," which was so exciting that it made you cry out "Oh!", and to be perfectly honest, I never really understood the "plane" part. But there you have it.

He set it on the ground and pointed his Bigging Machine at it and then pressed the bigging button.

He missed the Air Oh! Plane by at least six feet, and we ended up with a giant earthworm in our front yard instead. The worm was quite frightened at suddenly being so large, and it immediately burrowed back into the ground, causing an earthquake, and making a hole in our yard roughly the size of a small lake. It tunneled so quickly that we were unable to hit it with P's Shrinking Invention before it disappeared.

So if you happen to see an earthworm the size of a steam engine, now you know why. Sometimes we're a bit careless with our inventions. Sorry. I hope you're not scared of worms.

M took the Bigging Machine and pointed it at the Air Oh! Plane. Thankfully, her aim was much better than P's.

A few moments later, we were all climbing into the full sized Air Oh! Plane. I have to say, it felt good to be back in that wonderful invention. We had a lot of fun the last time we flew around the world. In fact, I would go so far as to call it the best time of my life.

I sat in my regular seat at the back of the plane, and found the "CAPTAIN" cap that my father had made for me. I put it on and smiled. P quickly took it from me and put a "FIRST MATE" cap on my head instead. P takes his caps very seriously, and he was clearly going to be the captain for this adventure.

M found an open bag of peanuts on her seat that she had brought on our last trip and was happy to learn that they were still fresh.

Suddenly, Rose screamed.

She hopped out of her seat and jumped onto one of the wings of the Air Oh! Plane. She was shaking like a hiccupping bowl full of jelly. We all looked over to her seat, and were confused at what we saw.

A little hairy head poked out, followed by a large pair of brown eyes.

"Is that what I think it is?" my father asked.

"I think so," M said in an astonished tone. "It's a monkey."

P turned to M.

"Oh, it's a monkey?" he said. "I thought it was a hairy baby."

I CHOKED

"It's a *saimiri sciureus*," M said, as she cracked one of her peanuts and gently offered it to the monkey.

"Really?" I said. "Because it looks more like a monkey to me."

"It *is* a monkey, but that's the scientific name of the species," Rose told me.

"Oh."

"I read all about these monkeys when we were traveling through South America," M said with a giggle as the monkey took the peanut from her hand and sniffed it. "They're referred to as 'common squirrel monkeys.'"

A *squirrel* monkey. Of course.

I sort of have a weird thing with squirrels. I don't really want to talk about it. So I'm not going to.

"We must have accidentally shrunk it in South America when we were shrinking things to take home as souvenirs," P said as he gently petted the common squirrel monkey on the head. "Poor thing. It's probably been living off these peanuts for the past few weeks."

M ran back to the Baron Estate to fetch some fresh fruit for the monkey to eat.

The monkey ate a few peanuts and then stared at my father. My father stared back. The monkey patted P's spiky hair. P patted the top of the monkey's head. P fed the monkey a peanut. The monkey fed P a peanut. The monkey crawled onto P's shoulder and began to pick at his hair. P began to pick at the monkey's hair. Then they looked at each other and slowly nodded their heads.

"I feel like this monkey understands me," P said.

It was true. Most people don't get along that well with my father.

M came back out with a basket filled with fresh fruit for the monkey. After it had eaten, it immediately fell asleep in P's arms.

"We'll have to return it to its home in South America," said M. "The poor thing probably misses its family."

P frowned. The monkey stirred, frowning in its sleep.

"Maybe we can return it to its home after we find the

treasure," P suggested. "I mean, we should start searching for that treasure right away. We made a promise to the President."

"To the *Vice* President," Rose corrected.

"It's still an important promise to an important person," P insisted, taking off his coat and wrapping it around the monkey like it actually was a hairy little baby. "Is everyone ready for takeoff? Our next stop is the Southern California coast. Once we're there, we'll shrink the Air Oh! Plane, and use the Bigging Machine on the underwater ship."

"I read that an underwater ship is called a 'submarine,'" I told him, feeling proud that I could teach my clever father something for once.

"Shhh," P shushed me. "The monkey is sleeping. Hmmmm . . . we can't very well go around calling it *the monkey*, can we? We should give it . . ." P peered at the sleeping monkey before continuing, "ah—*him*—a proper name."

"How about Squirrely?" Rose offered. "Since he's a squirrel monkey?"

P looked insulted by her suggestion.

"You're a girl," he said to Rose. "Would you like for us to call you Girly?"

". . . No."

"Then try to think of a better name for him."

"How about Benjamin?" M suggested, as she prepped the flying machine for takeoff. "We could name him after the President of the United States, Benjamin Harrison."

"That's not a bad idea," P said. "But I was thinking of naming him after my grandfather, Waldo. I've always wanted a son named Waldo."

"Um, you already have one. I'm your son. And I'm named Waldo."

"You don't count," P told me as he gently rocked the sleeping monkey back and forth. "You prefer to go by W.B."

"Ready for takeoff," M said as she started the Air Oh! Plane.

She flipped a switch and the propellers began to spin. As they spun, they made a wonderfully loud *thwapping* noise, and the tall grass surrounding us began to whip around in a wild frenzy. We all put on our goggles and leather flying caps, and as the Air Oh! Plane started to roll forward, out of the corner of my eye I saw an eggplant omelet running towards us.

It took me a moment to realize that it was Aunt Dorcas.

Which I suppose made more sense.

"Wait!" Aunt Dorcas screamed as she ran after the Air Oh! Plane. "Wait! Where are you going? You're not leaving me alone here again, are you?"

I turned to Rose.

"Did anyone tell Aunt Dorcas where we're going?" I yelled over the whirling of the propellers.

"We aren't supposed to tell anyone where we're going!" Rose yelled back. "Remember? We promised Vice President Morton that we would keep this a secret!"

"But won't she be worried about us?"

"Would you rather have her come along?"

"Good point."

"Wait!" Aunt Dorcas continued to yell, her purple face turning even purpler as she ran after the winged flying machine. "Where are you going? Answer me! Will you be back later today? Should I wait for you for supper? Where did you leave my foot medicine? Is that a mon-keeeeeeeeeeeeeeeyyyyyyyy . . ."

My eggy aunt's voice faded away as the Air Oh! Plane caught the winds and began its graceful climb into the sky. Rose and I waved goodbye to Aunt Dorcas, who continued to cry and scream even though we could no longer hear her.

"Was that Aunt Dorcas?" M asked as she wiped her

goggles and looked down at the slowly shrinking ground. "What did she want?"

"She just wanted to wish us a pleasant flight," I told M, and Rose nodded her head.

"Awww, that's nice," M said as she steered the flying Air Oh! Plane westward, pulling up until we were sailing over the fluffy summer clouds.

"*Lullaby, and goodnight,*" my father sang to Waldo. "*My sweet little mon-key. Close your eyes. Dream of flies. That you'll pick from your hair.*"

An hour later, we landed on the beautiful California coast. We sat there and watched as the breeze blew softly over the Pacific Ocean. The white foamed waves crept further and further up the sandy beach where we had parked, and the air was thick with the invigorating smell of salt water. After we climbed out of the Air Oh! Plane, my father shrunk it and placed it into a bag. He then pulled out his little submarine and tossed it into the sea. Before he could use his Bigging Machine on it, my mother gently took the invention from his hand.

"Why don't you let me do it, dear?" M said to him. "We don't want to accidentally create a giant sea monster."

"If that's what you wish, my little muffin," P responded stiffly, clearly upset by M's lack of faith in his aim. "I need to check on little Waldo anyway."

He peeled a peanut and fed it to little Waldo—and by "little Waldo," I mean the monkey, not me. I still had to peel my own peanuts.

Once M used the Bigging Machine on the submarine, we were able to see what a truly fantastic and detailed invention the underwater ship really was.

It was made almost completely out of metal, and it was covered with dozens of circular windows shaped like eyeballs. The body of the submarine looked sort of like a fat fish, with rubber and metal flippers sticking out of each side, which allowed the submarine to slowly paddle through the water like a giant sea turtle. There was a little hatch on top where you entered the submarine, and right in front of the hatch was a long metal tube with a rectangular piece of glass at the end.

"What's that?" Rose asked, pointing to the tube and the glass.

"It's a *periscope*," P answered. "We have plenty of windows in the submarine which will allow us to see what's happening around us in the water, but the periscope can be raised to allow us to see what's happening *above* the water."

There was a little ladder welded to the side, which we used to climb on top of the submarine. P opened the hatch and crawled inside with little Waldo perched on his shoulders. M followed, and then Rose and I did as well.

I don't know what I was expecting the inside of the submarine to look like. I suppose I assumed that it would look as plain and practical as the outside. But my father had surprised us all by designing the inside to look like the living room of a nice and ordinary home. It was really quite cozy. There was brightly colored wallpaper, cushioned sofas and chairs, a dining table, a kitchen corner with an ice box and a little stove, and another room with two comfortable looking sets of bunk beds stacked against the walls.

"Sharon and I will take the bunks on the left," P said. "And Rose and little Waldo can take the bunks on the right."

"You meant me, and not the monkey. Right, P?" I asked.

P glanced at me and bit his lip, looking very much like he'd forgotten that I was there.

"Of course I meant you," he said quickly. "I definitely meant you and not the monkey."

At the front of the submarine was a large rectangular

window, and underneath the window there was a little control panel with several metal cranks and levers and buttons. There was a metal steering wheel which P had taken from a rather awkward bathtub-helicopter invention he had built a few years earlier, an invention which M had refused to let him use (she said it was indecent to fly around the country while soaking in the tub).

P immediately went to the chair set up behind the steering wheel, and my mother went to the chair behind the control panel. M pressed a button and pulled a lever, and the submarine began to sink underwater. I watched as all of the little covered lanterns that P had built along the sides of the submarine lit up at once, giving us a clear view of what was happening under the sea.

Not a whole lot was happening. There was a ton of seaweed floating around. There were a few crabs scuttling along the ocean bottom, and a couple of bored looking fish. The fish spotted us and began to act as though they were doing something important, probably so we wouldn't think that fish spend all of their time floating around doing nothing.

I glared at the fish to let them know that I was on to them. Fish are lazy. Don't believe anyone who tells you differently.

"Would anyone like to have lunch before we leave?" Rose asked. "I know that I would. I haven't eaten since this morning."

"I'm hungry too," I said, though I was always hungry, and everyone knew that I was always hungry, so there really wasn't any need for me to say it.

"There's no time for lunch," P said, as he and M flipped a few switches on the control panel. "I want us pointed in the right direction and moving before we lose any more time."

Waldo the squirrel monkey shrieked loudly and pointed to his mouth. I don't speak monkey, but his large brown eyes seemed to say, "I need food! Now!"

P smiled.

"Oh, alright," he said, scooping up Waldo and carrying him to the kitchen corner. "I can't say no to you, my good little boy. Let's have lunch. I'll make the tastiest meal you've ever had, my lovely little Waldo, just for you."

I can't remember P ever making a tasty meal just for me.

Once lovely little Waldo and the rest of us had eaten, my father and mother fired up the submarine, activated the flippers, and started heading south.

Like the Flying Baron Estate (and by that I mean our house, which my parents had transformed into a flying machine for a race around the country last January), the submarine was steam powered, with a coal burning stove located near the back. All of the ship's coal was conveniently stored in a large, hidden compartment under the floor.

My parents had managed to invent something that pumped oxygen into the submarine through vents in the ceiling. M started explaining to me how they had done that, and I really tried to listen to her explanation, but then I spotted a funny looking fish out the window and I stopped paying attention.

In my defense, it was one of those skinny little fish that blows up into a big bubble when it's scared. The moment it saw the splendid Baron submarine, it blew up into a comically giant ball, and I was able to count all the little spiny bits on its body. It was pretty great.

While my father steered the submarine and my mother navigated, Rose and I sat beside one another on the sofa and stared out the windows at the secret underwater world, which seemed to grow more and more impressive the further we traveled.

The fish we saw were beautiful and unique, swimming around in their little schools as they searched for food. We passed by the remains of old shipwrecks, where sharks and eels swam and slithered through the splintered wood. Stingrays rose from the ground in a slow moving cloud of sand. Spiny lobsters crawled over rocks. I even saw a small family of seahorses dart by—cute little creatures that were no larger than my finger.

I wondered if I could use my father's Shrinking Invention to shrink myself small enough to ride one of those little seahorses like an underwater cowboy. It would probably be much safer than riding a real horse on land, because if I fell off the seahorse, I'd just float around in the water instead of landing on the hard ground. But then again, when riding a horse on land, there was very little chance that a large creature would appear out of nowhere and swallow me and my horse in a single bite. In the ocean, that was a very real possibility.

See? That's why I preferred not to get ideas. I should have been born a slug.

"It's incredible," Rose breathed. "It's like something out of a wild dream."

I usually dreamed about talking squirrels or giant sand-wiches that tried to eat me, but I still nodded my head in agreement. It was absolutely incredible, the most incredible thing I had ever seen.

And then I felt something land on top of my head. A sharp pair of nails dug into my scalp. Something stuck the end of its tail into my ear and began to poke around.

"Waldo?" I said.

Waldo responded by taking two of his tiny monkey fingers and poking me in both of my eyes.

"Ow!"

Then he hopped down beside me and gave me a little shove. I forced myself to smile at him and then looked back out the window. The monkey shoved me again. And then again. Waldo shrieked into my ear and then shoved me one more time.

"What does he want?" I asked Rose through gritted teeth.

"I think you're in his spot," she answered with a giggle.

"But I was here first."

Waldo shoved me yet again. I stood up, and the little monkey immediately sat in my spot. He then nudged me away so I wouldn't block his view out the window. I shot him an angry look, but then he shot me an even angrier one.

I sat on the floor beside the sofa.

"Lousy, stupid monkey . . ."

The submarine didn't travel nearly as fast as the Air Oh! Plane, but it still moved fast enough for us to see some amazing things. At one point, we joined a pod of whales which were traveling south. The whales were really quite friendly. They sang us their loud whale songs, which made the entire metal submarine vibrate. One of the mother whales sort of adopted us, which was slightly awkward when she tried to cuddle up to us during a nap. When she started trying to feed us, we knew that it was time to go our separate ways.

My father regularly used the periscope to see what was happening on the surface of the sea, and sometimes he would let us look through it as well. Usually we saw nothing but big choppy waves. Once I looked through it and saw a huge eyeball. It made me scream. My scream woke up Waldo, who got angry and bit me on the head. I told my father about it, complaining that his monkey wasn't very nice to me.

"Well he says that you're not very nice to him either," P responded. "Don't make me choose sides between my children, W.B., that's not fair."

"But he's not your child. He's just a monkey!"

I looked over at Waldo who glared at me from beneath the bill of his "FIRST MATE" cap. Actually, it was *my* "FIRST MATE" cap, but P had given it to Waldo after claims that the monkey's head was getting cold.

I was glad that I brought my books with me, because after the first week or so of slowly paddling along in the deepest part of the ocean, I began to grow a bit bored staring out the window. Rose spent a lot of time with my parents, learning how the submarine worked and how to operate it, but I wasn't particularly interested in any of that. You could tell me that the submarine was powered by fairy burps and leprechaun spit, and I'd probably believe it. And my parents knew better than to let me steer anything –I once crashed a bicycle that wasn't even moving.

So I spent most of my time reading.

Of course, I only had three books left which I could still read, because the rest of my books had been ripped apart by little Waldo, who was quickly becoming my worst enemy. In fact, I was starting to hate that monkey with a passion. I hated him more than I'd ever hated another living thing, including the kid at school who stole my liverwurst sandwich and replaced the liverwurst with . . . well, let's just say that now I double-check what's in my sandwiches before I eat them.

Little Waldo would wake me up in the morning by

pulling my eyelids open and screaming in my face. He'd also steal my food, take my seat, mess up my bed, flick my ears, lick my drinking glass, use my toothbrush, stretch out my socks, and sometimes he'd creep up behind one of my parents or Rose and then shove the back of their heads. When they'd turn around to see who shoved them, he'd jump out of the way and point at me, like I was the one who did it. And for some reason, they always believed him. Apparently I'm less believable than a monkey.

"Quit shoving my head, W.B.," Rose had said after Waldo had shoved the back of her head and then pointed at me. "Or I'll shove you back."

"It wasn't me!" I claimed. "It was the monkey!"

Rose rolled her eyes.

"You're always blaming everything on Waldo. But he's a perfectly sweet little monkey."

She looked over at little Waldo, who gave her a perfectly sweet little monkey smile, as though he was a hairy angel who never did anything wrong. When she looked away, he stuck his little monkey tongue out at me. I shook my fist at him. He shook his fist back at me. We continued shaking our fists at each other until suppertime.

It was day fourteen on our trip to the South Pacific. We had surfaced earlier that morning, so that we could bathe in the warmth of the sun and get some much needed fresh air. When we climbed out of the hatch and sat on top of the metal submarine, we had nothing to look at but the open sea. We couldn't see land, and we couldn't see any other ships. It felt like we were the only people (and monkey) left in the world. It was a very lonely feeling.

Everyone was beginning to grow a bit grumpy. And by a bit, I mean A LOT. Fourteen days is a long time to spend in a little submarine with nothing to do but stare at the sea, which was no longer as magical and entertaining as it was before. In fact, I was starting to hate all of the stupid fish and dolphins and turtles and whales and seals that we saw out the windows. I'd make faces at them as we passed, stretching out my mouth with my fingers while I stuck out my tongue. The sea creatures tried to make faces back, but since they didn't have fingers to stretch out their mouths, they couldn't makes ones as good as me. Score one for W.B.

"Remind me again why we couldn't have flown to the island in the Air Oh! Plane?" Rose Blackwood asked M and P as we reentered the submarine and closed the hatch. "Why did we have to ride in this slow little tin can the whole way there?"

"We didn't know if there would be a good place on the island to land the Air Oh! Plane," M told her. "And this *little tin can* is a wonderful invention, which was our best option for safely getting to the island, and then searching for the treasure in the surrounding waters. You didn't have to come along if you didn't want to, Rose. We would have been alright with you staying home with Aunt Dorcas."

She said it in a biting tone which I could tell hurt Rose's feelings.

"She's right," P said. "You didn't have to come along, Rose. Neither did you, W.B."

"Me?" I exclaimed. "Why did you mention me? I didn't even say anything!"

"You've been giving Waldo a hard time for the past two weeks, and it's very upsetting. You and Rose are trying to make little Waldo and me miserable!"

"Oh, stop talking about your silly monkey!" M snapped at P. "I wish we would have never decided to take him along with us. He smells terrible."

"So does W.B.!" P insisted.

"Again, why are you picking on me? I didn't even say

anything!"

"Oh, you never say or do anything wrong, do you, W.B.?" Rose said to me in a mocking tone. "Nothing is ever your fault, is it? It's the monkey who keeps shoving everyone's head, right? I swear, you are so whiny and ridiculous, with your nonstop fimble-fambles."

"Fimble-fambles? *Fimble-fambles???!!!*"

If I knew what that meant, I probably would have been *really* upset by it.

"It's true, he is pretty darn whiny," P agreed.

"You two need to leave W.B. alone!" M shouted.

Waldo shrieked loudly, letting everyone know that he was upset as well.

"Oh, shut up, you!" I yelled at the monkey. "I wish we'd never unshrunk you!"

"W.B.! Apologize to Waldo for that!" my father demanded.

"I'm not apologizing to a monkey!"

"I wish I hadn't come along!" Rose moaned.

"I wish Vice President Morton hadn't convinced us to search for this dumb treasure!" P snarled.

"I wish the monkey could take a bath!" M groaned.

"I wish we could turn around and go home," I grunted.

Waldo bit me on the head.

That was it. That was the straw that broke the camel's back. I don't know why people use that particular expression (Why are you carrying so much straw to begin with? Why are you only using one camel to carry it? Who's going to take care of the camel now that it's injured? I think you owe the camel an apology, don't you?), but I knew that I was sick and tired of little Waldo, and I could no longer control my temper.

"Alright, you!" I growled as I stood up and tried to grab Waldo. "Now it's time for me to rearrange your ugly, little monkey face!"

Waldo shrieked at me as he bounced from chair to chair, scampering up the walls and swinging from the pipes that ran across the ceiling. I continued to chase him even though I kept slipping and tripping and falling with every other step.

"W.B., stop chasing my monkey!" P said angrily. "That's an order from your captain!"

"You're not my captain!" I told him as I dove at Waldo. "You gave away my 'FIRST MATE' cap!"

"Waldo's head was cold!"

"He's a monkey!" my mother said as she rolled her eyes. "His head wasn't cold. You just wanted to see a monkey in a hat because you thought it would be funny and cute.

W.B., stop chasing Waldo. Otherwise you're going to—"

M didn't finish her sentence, but I assume she was going to tell me that if I kept chasing Waldo, I might crash into something and break it.

Because that's exactly what happened next.

I ran into the coal burning stove, which ripped cleanly from the wall. A long pipe coming out of the top of the stove bent and snapped, cutting off the power to the submarine. Several of the turning gears in the walls jammed and twanged as springs shot out like pellets from a rifle. I could feel the submarine come to an immediate stop. We slowly started to sink until we landed on the ocean floor.

Everyone looked at me. P scratched his head. M buried her face in her hands. Rose's chin quivered.

I had broken the submarine.

Before I could apologize, the vent on the side of the stove suddenly sprayed me in the face with a huge puff of black ash.

"Lousy, stupid monkey," I choked.

I Quickly Curled Up and Pretended To Be a Shell

For a moment, no one spoke. No one moved. No one even blinked. It was almost as though they couldn't believe what had just happened. Or maybe they thought that if they held really still without speaking, then somehow everything would magically fix itself and the submarine would no longer be broken. That seemed like a good idea, so I decided to hold still while remaining silent as well.

When a situation seems hopeless, you can always choose to be in denial about it.

Then I sneezed. The ash from the stove had irritated my nose. My eyes suddenly burned so badly that I could hardly see. I squeezed them tightly shut, and ran my knuckles over my sooty eyelids.

"Here," I heard M say. "Wipe your face with this towel, W.B."

With my eyes blinded by the ash, I reached out and immediately felt something bite my fingers.

"Ow!" I cried. "Lousy, stupid monkey! Wait, that was the monkey, right?"

"Yes," Rose said bitterly. "But I sort of feel like biting you too. We're trapped at the bottom of the ocean because of you, W.B."

I found my mother's towel and used it to wipe the ash from my face and neck.

"So what do we do now?" I asked.

P scratched his head with one hand while he scratched his chin with the other hand. I had noticed he'd been very itchy lately.

"I suppose I could try tinkering with the pipes and the gears and the springs and the stove to see if I can fix them . . ." he began, ". . . but I don't know if that will work. I don't have many of my tools with me."

"I don't think the lack of tools is the problem," M frowned as she inspected the busted pipe. "You need to replace this entire pipe and several of the gears, and frankly, I don't think we have enough scrap metal to do that. Tinkering won't help if we don't have enough materials. We need replacement metal."

Uh oh.

"How much oxygen do we have?" Rose asked, suddenly looking very pale. "Is there a chance that we'll run out of air down here?"

"We have quite a bit of oxygen left," M told her quickly. "Please don't start to panic, Rose. Panicking is the worst thing we can do at a time like this."

"Can't we just make the Air Oh! Plane big again?" I asked P. "We could fly the rest of the way to the island, or fly home and build a new submarine."

P shook his head.

"The Air Oh! Plane will be damaged if we use the Bigging Machine on it while it's under the sea. It wasn't meant to go in the water. The wings and propellers are too delicate. Plus, it has to roll and pick up speed before it can fly, so it needs to be on solid land."

"What we need is a miracle," Rose said quietly.

Everyone went silent again as we hoped for a miracle. As I hoped as hard as I could hope, I happened to look out one of the windows of the submarine. I spotted something shiny on the ocean floor.

"What's that?" I asked, pointing to the shiny something.

My parents and Rose went to windows and looked. While they were turned away, Waldo shoved me again, and then ran away before I could shove him back.

"Why . . . it looks like a wrecked steamship," P said, his eyes growing wide with excitement. "That's perfect! If we can take some of the metal from the steamship and bring it in here, I could reshape it to fix the pipes and the gears and the stove!"

"But how would you do that?" M asked. "How can you bring that metal into our submarine? It's out there, and we're trapped in here."

"Hmmmmm . . ."

P sat on the floor and thought.

My father didn't think like most people. Most people think by standing there with a look of concentration on their face, or maybe they need to pace for a bit. But in order to think, P needed to sit cross-legged on the floor, and he needed to close one eye, and he needed to stick up his thumbs, and he needed to poke his tongue out of the corner of his mouth, and he needed to puff out his cheeks.

Basically, he needed to sit there like a confused gargoyle that looked as though it was about to throw up. Like most things about my father, it was very weird. But it always seemed to work.

"I've got it!" he finally cried, springing up and rushing to the little closet beside our bunks. He opened the closet door and rummaged through it, moving aside the extra clothes and blankets and pillows, and eventually he pulled out a little rubber suit and a large oval helmet. The helmet appeared to be made of glass. It had a hose attached to the back of it, a long, coiled hose which was hooked onto some sort of pump. It looked very strange, like something that a creature from another planet would wear while visiting earth.

"What in the world is that?" Rose asked.

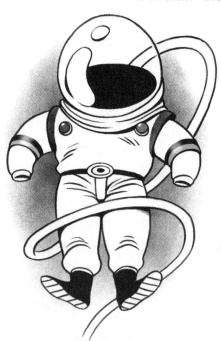

"It's an underwater breathing suit!" P said proudly. "It's attached to a pump which will provide oxygen to the person wearing the suit. The helmet is made of a new material that I accidentally created when I spilled some chemicals into my morning oatmeal.

It tasted awful, in case you were wondering, but it's as clear as glass and ten times as strong. I had almost forgotten that I invented this suit a few months earlier, and placed it in here to use in case of an underwater emergency. If I put on this suit, I'll be able to breathe underwater, which means I can leave the submarine and collect the scrap metal from that shipwreck. We'll be saved!"

But before we could all begin to cheer, P held up the underwater suit and frowned.

While it was true that the underwater suit and helmet might solve our problem, it was clearly too small for P to wear. In fact, it was so small that only two of us in the submarine could possibly fit into it. And one of us was a monkey.

Everyone looked at me. I looked at little Waldo, who quickly shook his monkey head, letting me know that I was on my own.

"W.B.," my father said with an apologetic look on his face, "you're the only one small enough to fit into the suit. I'm afraid that *you'll* have to be the one who leaves the submarine and collects the scrap metal from the shipwreck."

!!!

For a moment, I was speechless.

My father wanted me, a kid who was so clumsy that he

once got his nose stuck in the bathtub drain, to walk across the ocean floor all by myself, where I'd be at the mercy of the sea serpents and octopi and angry mermaids.

I quickly thought of an excuse to get out of it.

"Can't you just use your Bigging Machine to make the suit a little bit larger so it'll fit you?"

P shook his head as he scratched behind his ears like a dog.

"That's not the way the Bigging Machine works, W.B. We already used the Bigging Machine on the suit once when we *biggened* the submarine, which means that the suit is already *bigged*. You can't *biggen* something twice with the Bigging Machine, otherwise it will just become crumbly and fall apart. In fact, I wrote quite clearly in the instruction manual for the Bigging Machine: Never, ever *biggen* a *bigged biggened* thing.'"

"You're all aware that *biggened*, *bigged*, and *biggen* aren't real words, right?" Rose asked everyone.

"Not now, Rose," M whispered.

"What if you shrunk yourself to fit into the suit, P?" I asked, looking out the window and into the very dark and terrifying sea. "You still have your Shrinking Invention."

"That won't work either," said P as he scratched his neck, grunting with discomfort. "The Shrinking Invention has only one setting, and that's the *squirrel* setting. I can only use it to shrink myself to the size of a squirrel, not to the size of a six-year-old boy."

"I'm eleven."

"It doesn't matter."

P held the suit up to me. It was clearly a perfect fit. It almost looked as though it'd been made specifically for me. I stared out the window again and shivered. There were all sorts of dangerous creatures at the bottom of the ocean, creatures which would view a kid like me as a delicious treat. In the submarine I felt protected, but out there, with only a rubber suit and a helmet, I'd be as helpless as a floating hamburger.

"How would I even get out there?" I argued. "If we open up the hatch, it will flood the inside of the submarine. You'll all drown."

"There's a little room in the back the submarine," P told me as he scratched at his eyebrows and ear hairs. "That room has a door with a waterproof seal on it. Once you're in there with the door closed, I can press a button on the control panel. The back of the submarine will open, and let you out without flooding the rest of the submarine. After you've collected some scrap metal, then you can swim into the backroom and knock on the door. Then I can close the back of the submarine and drain all the water from the room before letting you inside with the rest of us."

"That's very clever, Mr. Baron," Rose told my father.

"Yes, McLaron, very clever," M said, and then she gave him a kiss on the cheek.

Little Waldo hopped onto my father's shoulder and gave his head a hug, and then began to pick at the tiny bugs in P's hair. Everyone was so happy with how clever my father was that they had completely overlooked one simple problem with the plan.

Me.

"I don't want to do it," I told them. "And you can't make me."

"Oh yes, we can," said M.

"Oh no, you can't," I replied.

"Oh yes, we can," said P.

"Oh no, you can't," I answered.

"Oh yes, we can," said Rose.

"Oh no, you—"

The next thing I knew, I was suddenly dressed in the underwater suit and standing in the back room of the submarine.

". . . How did that just happen?"

"Good luck, W.B.!" P called to me from the control

panel.

"Be careful not to overexert yourself out there!" M added. "Otherwise, it might be devastating to your system! Be calm! Move slowly and cautiously, W.B., and be mindful of hyperventilating! That could cause severe trauma to your brain!"

"What does 'hyperventilating' mean?" I yelled.

M, who couldn't hear me, just waved to me and smiled, before turning to the control panel.

"I believe in you!" Rose shouted.

Waldo screamed something at me, and even though I don't speak monkey, I'm pretty sure he was trying to say, "I hope you get eaten by a big ugly sea monster!"

The metal door closed in my face, locking me in the back room of the submarine. I stared pathetically through the little round window in the door, trying to make my family take pity on me with my sad and desperate eyes. I'm not good at a lot of things, but I'm pretty darn good at looking sad and desperate.

The back of the submarine began to open, the wall slowly disappearing and allowing the seawater to pour inside. I turned around and pounded on the door, pleading with my family to open up and let me back into the submarine, even though I knew that at that point they wouldn't be able to. The water quickly filled the open room.

It was strange being able to breathe in a room full of water, and it was also pretty amazing. I was able to appreciate what a wonderful invention the underwater suit really was. I took deep breaths of fresh air as I jumped up and slowly floated through the water, feeling very much like a bubble-headed fish. It was almost like flying, only better, since it would be almost impossible for me to crash land.

And then I looked out into the open sea ahead of me.

I almost fainted with fear.

I turned around and pounded on the metal door until my fists hurt. Then I kicked it until my toes hurt. And then I head butted it until I realized that it probably wouldn't be a good thing if my helmet cracked.

I sighed. It looked as though I had no choice but to do what I was told.

Using my feet to push off from the door, I propelled myself out of the submarine and into the open sea. The lights mounted on the outside of the submarine allowed me to see everything in our general area, but everything beyond was covered in darkness. Terrible, horrible, knee-knockingly, teeth-chatteringly, pants-wettingly scary darkness. Anything could be out there. And there was nothing I found more frightening than anything.

The tube that ran out of the top of my helmet not only gave me air, it also attached me to the oxygen pump that P had locked into place in the backroom of the submarine, so I wouldn't get lost. Of course, if that tube was cut, not only would I be lost, I'd also be without air . . . which probably wouldn't be a good thing. I like air quite a lot. In fact, it's one of my favorite things to breathe.

I'm not a particularly good swimmer, but that didn't seem to matter. The rubber suit was weighted, which meant I could just walk across the ocean floor to the shipwreck, occasionally jumping up and flying in slow motion as I paddled with my arms and kicked with my legs, which was actually sort of fun.

Once I reached the shipwreck, I noticed a long sheet of metal stuck into the ground, and so I began to dig around it. As I dug, I realized for the first time that there weren't any fish around, not by the submarine or by the shipwreck. In fact, the whole area seemed to be completely free of fish, despite the fact that there were slimy little plants sticking out from the ground, the sort of slimy plants that tiny fish usually enjoyed nibbling on.

That seemed rather odd, but I was a little too nervous and distracted to spend too much time focusing on odd things. To be perfectly honest, there are so many odd things in my life that if I actually took the time to focus on them all, I'd never have time to do anything else.

After I had dug up most of the metal sheet, I began to pull on it, slowly extracting it from the sand. That was harder than I thought it would be, but I somehow managed it, and somehow I did it without hurting myself, which was nothing short of a miracle.

I carried the metal sheet into the open room at the back of the submarine. After I had set it on the ground, I knocked on the door so they could let me back in. My father's face appeared at the little round window, and looked down at me. I pointed to the metal sheet that I'd found. He looked at it and frowned, before pulling out his notepad and pencil. He quickly jotted something onto the pad, and then held it up to the window.

"GET MORE", the paper said.

I shook my head no.

P nodded his head yes.

I shook my head no.

P nodded his head yes.

I wanted to shake my head again, but shaking my head in the underwater suit was starting to make me dizzy.

P put down the paper and mouthed that I was doing a good job while scratching the crown of his head with both hands. M and Rose leaned into the window and smiled, mouthing that they were proud of me. When they had left, Waldo's little monkey face appeared at the window. For a moment he just stared at me, and then he blew a raspberry with his tongue, before turning around and shaking his little monkey backside at me.

Lousy, stupid, sassy monkey . . .

I walked back to the area surrounding the shipwreck and searched for more loose metal. I couldn't find any more metal in the sand, so I decided to check inside the ship. A huge hole had been ripped into the side of it, presumably from the crash that had caused it to sink. With a jump so graceful that I could hardly believe it was done by me, I made my way inside.

The inside of the ship was covered in seaweed and sea grass and other slimy sea stuff which I couldn't identify, even if you gave me a year to do so. I really don't like touching slimy things. I have never in my life heard of a good thing that's happened to someone as a result of touching a slimy thing. No one that I know has ever said "Oh boy! There's some slippery and slimy goop on my hand! Huzzah!"

As I was exploring the remains of the ship, my hand scraped against something sharp. I saw that I had cut my finger. I tried to do what I normally did when I cut myself, which was to put my cut finger inside my mouth. But the stupid helmet got in the way. It was probably for the best. The last thing I wanted was a mouth full of salt water and slime.

I finally discovered some more loose scrap metal further inside the sunken ship, and went to work collecting it. I wasn't sure how much metal P and M needed to repair the submarine, so I decided to grab all the metal that I could carry. After I had taken three large pieces and two small pieces and stuck them under my arm, I looked up and found myself staring into the third ugliest face I'd ever seen.

In case you're curious, the second ugliest face I'd ever seen belonged to Weasel Face, or Veezlefayce, or whatever his name was. And the ugliest face I'd ever seen belonged to a man from Nevada named Spud Spuddlesworth. He had a face that only a mother could love, assuming that mother had been born without eyeballs.

But while this face wasn't as ugly as their faces, it was far more dangerous and frightening. It was the face of a giant eel, with yellow eyes and sharp looking teeth. It whipped its body around as it showed me those sharp looking teeth, flashing me the evilest grin I'd ever seen.

"Good eel," I said cautiously as I slowly backed away, hoping that what eels liked more than anything was compliments. "Nice eel. Pretty eel. Gentle eel. Lovely eel teeth you have there. Very long and pointy looking."

As I backed away, I felt the backside of my rubber suit bump into something solid that I didn't remember being there before.

When I turned around, I saw that it was a giant shark. A giant and hungry looking shark.

The shark stared at me. I stared at the shark.

"C'mon!" I said to the shark as I pointed to the eel. "Let's get him!"

But the shark wasn't interested in the eel, and the eel wasn't interested in the shark. They were both only interested in me, the weakest and tastiest one there.

The shark and the eel slowly began to close in on me. They both looked quite hungry. And, just my luck, I happened to look absolutely delicious in my little rubber suit.

It appeared to me that there was only one thing left that I could do.

I quickly curled up and pretended to be a shell.

A MONKEY WATCHING
HUMANS ACT LIKE APES

I thought my plan was pretty clever, until I heard the sound of shark teeth tapping against my helmet. When I looked up, I saw both the shark and the eel shaking their heads at me, letting me know that I hadn't fooled them. I shrugged and smiled.

"Can't blame a fella for trying, right?"

Apparently, they *could* blame a fella for trying, since they both lunged at me with their mouths wide open. One of them likely would have taken a large bite out of me if they hadn't accidentally bonked their heads together.

I laughed at the stunned looks on their faces but quickly realized that it might not be a good idea to laugh at something that's trying to eat you.

They both pouted for a moment, embarrassed by their underwater clumsiness, but their embarrassment quickly transformed into rage.

"Uh oh," I said, and then I pointed behind them. "Look! Over there! An even bigger and slower kid for you to eat!"

When they turned around, I put my feet against the side of the wrecked steamship and pushed off, sending myself shooting through the water in the direction of the submarine. When I began to slow down, I kicked my feet and paddled with my arm that wasn't carrying the scrap metal, attempting to swim the rest of the way back.

I wasn't going very fast. In fact, I wasn't really going anywhere at all. I was just sort of spinning around in a circle. My heart was racing, and I was breathing so hard that I was actually fogging up the inside of my helmet. I remembered what M had told me about "hyperventilating." I wasn't sure what that meant, but it sounded like something that had to do with breathing. My brain told me that since I was underwater, I would need to breathe twice as fast and twice as hard as I normally do, so that's what I did.

As I spun and breathed quickly, I saw the eel and the shark staring at me with expressions of disbelief on their faces. They looked at one another and shook their heads again. The eel said something to the shark. The shark laughed.

"Hey!" I called angrily over my shoulder as I continued to spin and pant. "It's rude to make fun of people behind their back!"

They waited until I had spun around and was facing them again before they made another joke about my swimming, and then they had another good laugh.

It was still pretty hurtful, but at least it was more polite.

The shark and the eel then decided to charge me again. They both had the same clever idea of going for my head, but, unfortunately for them, my head was the best protected part of me. Their teeth met the glassy material with a loud *CLANG!* which echoed inside my helmet like a bell.

But it also knocked me backwards in the direction of the submarine.

"Is that the best that you can do?" I called to the sea creatures with a pant, as I continued to float closer and closer to the open entrance of the backroom. "It feels like I'm being attacked by guppies! Tiny, little, baby guppies!"

The shark and the eel both charged at me again. I lowered my helmet, and this time when their jaws crashed into me, they knocked me only a few feet away from the submarine. I was now close enough to walk right in, knock on the inside door, and say goodbye to my underwater nightmare for good.

My nonstop, fast breathing appeared to be working. I was suddenly overcome with a total sense of calm. My brain was firing on all cylinders, instead of the one rusty and squeaky cylinder it usually fired on. Suddenly, I felt like the smartest kid in the world, and it was all thanks to my fast breathing. Maybe that's been my problem all along. I just haven't been breathing enough. I'd have to remember that when I got back on land. It looked like science would once again save the day. Good old hyperventilation.

"I'll see you later, guys!" I called to the confused looking shark and eel. "Probably at the end of a hook! Or maybe on a dinner plate! Heh heh heh . . ."

I chuckled to myself as I entered the back of the submarine and walked towards the door, but I stopped laughing when I felt an eel tail whip me on the backside. I slowly fell forward and bonked my head on the metal floor. This time when I bonked my head, I heard a light crunching sound.

At first I was confused, but then I saw the fine line of a long and splintered crack forming across the front of my helmet.

". . . Uh oh."

Recognizing the fact that I was weakening, the shark darted forward and tried to take another bite of me, its multiple rows of teeth scraping against the helmet, causing the crack to widen.

"Stop that!" I cried through my quick breaths. "If this helmet breaks, my hair will get wet!"

I backed into the door and knocked on it as hard as I could.

My father's face appeared at the little round window. When he saw the giant eel and the shark behind me, he started screaming. He rushed back to the control panel and tried to close the back end of the submarine, so he could drain the room that I was in and allow me back inside.

I suppose P thought that when the back of the submarine began to close, the sea creatures would panic and immediately swim out so they wouldn't be trapped. But that's not what happened. As the back of the submarine began to close, the shark stuck out its tail and blocked it. And since it couldn't close all the way, the back of the submarine slowly began to open again. My father must have invented some sort of clever safety feature which would protect people from getting crushed by the back of the submarine if they happened to be in the way of it while it was closing.

"Lousy, stupid, clever safety feature . . ." I muttered, hating the fact that my parents' inventions were all so annoyingly brilliant.

The creatures looked from my cracked helmet to my

rubber suit, and for the first time they realized that there were other parts of me that they could try biting, parts of me which wouldn't be as hard and unpleasant. The shark licked its lips, even though it didn't have lips. The eel drooled, which is rather difficult to do underwater.

I looked at my body and wondered which part of me they were planning to eat first. I would probably go for my left leg if I were them, though I can't quite say why. I took another step backwards, got tangled in my oxygen tube, and fell.

Falling underwater is rather strange because you do it at less than half the speed you do on land. So as I slowly fell to the floor, I noticed one of the smaller pieces of scrap metal that I had dropped. It looked quite sharp. After I landed on the ground, I picked it up and pointed it at the shark and the eel.

They found that pretty funny. I suppose I would too if I were them. After all, they had sharp teeth, as well as great strength and underwater speed, and here I was, a silly little land creature who could barely swim. In fact, it was so funny, that I started to laugh as well, wildly and uncontrollably, the sort of laughter that actually hurts your stomach and your brain. The shark and the eel swam over to me, daring me to stab them with the sharp piece of metal, presenting me with their fishy faces so I could have a free shot.

My hyperventilated brain then gave me a great idea. If *land* creatures grew smarter with more oxygen, then *sea* creatures would likely grow stupider with more oxygen! It made perfect sense! Because . . . well . . . because of opposites!

I took the sharp piece of metal . . . and used it to cut the oxygen tube attached to my helmet.

As my oxygen was cut off, a stream of powerful oxygen bubbles began to pour out from the end of the tube. I pointed the tube into the suddenly shocked faces of the eel and the shark. They both silently screamed before spinning around and swimming out of the backroom as quickly as they could. They found the intense bubbles pouring from the tube to be terrifying and unpleasant, and I can't say that I blamed them. No one likes having bubbles blown into their face. They must have been terrified by the effects of opposite hyperventilation.

With the outer door closed and the seawater drained from the little backroom of the submarine, my parents were finally able to open the door to let me back in.

The moment I stepped inside, they both wrapped their arms around me so tightly that my ears popped and my eyeballs bulged out. I knew they were talking to me because I could see their mouths moving, but I couldn't hear what they were saying because my ears were ringing too loudly. When they had finished hugging me, Rose Blackwood rushed over and did the same. There were tears in her eyes as she spoke to me, but I couldn't hear a single word that came out of her mouth.

I was also feeling really woozy. I'm guessing it's because I had almost been eaten by two of the scariest creatures I'd ever seen, while trapped at the bottom of the sea, with only an untested experiment providing me with oxygen. But I could be wrong. Maybe I just need more vitamins and exercise or something.

When everyone had finished hugging me, I pulled off the cracked helmet and took a deep breath. The room was spinning, and I was seeing double. No, make that triple. No, never mind. It was double. Quadruple? What's it called when you see five of something? It was that plus two. Actually, I was so dizzy that I couldn't really tell how many of anything I was seeing. I was too discombobulated to count. Maybe some hyperventilating would help. I took a few quick breaths, and nearly toppled over.

"Well?" the three (maybe four? Two? Six and a half?) Roses said to me. "Do you?"

"Huh?" I said as I rubbed my blurry eyes. "Do I what? Hold still, Roses. Stop spinning around. All nine of you."

"My poor son!" M cried, pulling me in for another big

hug. "You were so brave out there, W.B.! Please forgive us for risking your life."

"Oh. Sure."

I suppose I would have agreed to anything at that point. My brain felt as though had been churned into butter and slathered over a piece of sourdough toast, which reminded me that I was actually feeling pretty hungry.

"Your eyes look strange," M said with a frown as she opened my eyelids and examined my eyeballs. "Did you hear what I said about hyperventilating?"

"Yup. I did a whole lot of fast breathing, just like you told me to. It worked pretty well at first. It helped my brain come up with a way to outsmart those sea beasts. Oh, look. Pretty lights . . . pretty lights . . ."

"That's not what I meant," M said, suddenly looking very concerned. "Hyperventilating is when you breathe at a rapid rate, often while panicking, and that's precisely what I *didn't* want you to do. Just . . . breathe normally, W.B., and . . . oh dear."

She went to the kitchen corner to fetch me a glass of water. She was shaking her head and mumbling to herself. She must have been so proud of me for my quick thinking.

"I'm so sorry, my son," P said sadly. "I've been such a fool. Such an awful, terrible, brilliant fool."

"Oh . . . that's okay. Do we have any butter? And maybe a slice of toast or two? Or nine? Wait, how many are in a baker's dozen? I'd like that many. Plus one."

I heard a sniveling noise and spotted little Waldo sitting alone on the floor. He looked so sad that I might have felt bad for him if I didn't hate him so much.

"We put you into danger after treating you horribly," P said to me as he placed his hand on my shoulder. "And I've been treating you worse than anyone. I'm so sorry, son. Please forgive me."

"Oh . . ." I said again, and then I realized that I was saying "oh" quite a lot and should probably say something else. "Well, that's alright. I guess. Nothing out there ate me, so I suppose everything is hunky dory. Say, does anyone else hear that loud ringing noise?"

Chimes were clanging in my head, and my legs suddenly felt like wet noodles. I realized that I was swaying back and forth, and I began to wonder if I was about to fall over.

Yes. I was about to fall over. The weight of my large and ringing head was too much for my wobbly body to support, and as I slowly began to fall backwards, I prepared my body for an unpleasant meeting with the floor.

"Maybe you should sit down, W.B.," Rose said as she

caught me. "You're turning a weird shade of green."

Sitting down seemed like a good idea. My tongue felt like it was vibrating, and my eyes kept spinning in circles. With Rose's help, I sat on the sofa. M handed me a glass of water and once again told me that hyperventilating was a terrible thing to do, and that I was lucky it hadn't gotten me killed. Then she began to fill my aching head with all of the scientific reasons why hyperventilating hadn't given me my good idea to use the bubbles to frighten the sea creatures, while I nodded my throbbing head and pretended to listen to her.

As M lectured, Waldo slowly crawled over to me.

"No!" my father shouted sternly.

I sighed, and started to stand, assuming that I must have sat in the monkey's spot again.

But it turned out that P was shouting at Waldo, not at me.

"You leave him alone!" P said, shaking his finger at Waldo. "That's a bad little monkey!"

"Huh?" I said.

Rose sat down beside me and put her arm over my shoulder as she explained. "Mr. Baron is angry at the monkey now, for being mean to you, and also for eating the rest of our food, and especially for giving him fleas. Though

Mr. Baron denies having fleas."

"I don't have fleas!" P told us, as he scratched his head and chin and face and neck and arms. "I'm just a bit itchy. My hair and face must be tickling me. That's all. It's just a typical ticklish face episode. They happen all the time!"

"Waldo also jumped onto the control panel when Mr. Baron was trying to let you back into the submarine," Rose continued. "It's funny. It almost seemed like the monkey *wanted* you to stay out there with the shark and the eel."

I turned to the squirrel monkey as I unbuttoned my rubber suit. Waldo winced, as though he thought I might try to hit him.

"You're an evil little monkey," I whispered.

Tears started to form in the corner of the monkey's eyes. His bottom lip trembled as he bowed his head. He looked as though he was terribly sorry for what he'd done, and he quietly crawled into a dark corner of the submarine.

"I think we'll be letting little Waldo go as soon as we get to the island," P said, as he and my mother began to repair the pipe and the gears. "He's already caused us more than enough trouble."

"W.B., once again, I can't tell you how sorry we are," M told me. "And we're very proud of you for everything that you've done for us. Even if I'm sometimes baffled by your total misunderstanding of basic science."

Rose gave my shoulder another squeeze then helped me out of my rubber underwater suit.

"That's the bravest thing I've ever seen, W.B.," she told me. "You really deserve that medal."

I looked down at my WORLD'S GREATEST GRANDMA medal and grinned.

My parents and Rose were able to fix the submarine with the scrap metal, and soon we were back on course for the nameless little island in the South Pacific. P put on his captain's cap and continued to steer, while M served as his navigator. Rose filled the stove with coal and helped my mother to work the control panel.

I threw a blanket over my shoulders as I nestled into the sofa with one of my pirate adventure novels and a warm cup of tea.

From the corner of the submarine, I heard the soft and pitiful sound of a common squirrel monkey weeping.

It wasn't just another squirrel dream. It was *the mother of all squirrel dreams*. I was back in my underwater suit, walking slowly across the bottom of the sea. But this time I wasn't alone. There were three other people in underwater suits walking beside me, people who I naturally assumed were my parents and Rose. We were walking across the ocean floor in search of Captain Affect's lost treasure when suddenly I tripped and fell.

But I didn't fall in the slow and graceful way that a person falls while they're underwater. I fell in the fast and clumsy (and all too familiar) way that a person did when they were back on land. I realized that we weren't underwater. I removed my helmet and discovered that we were actually in the desert.

"Hey!" I called to the others. "We don't need these helmets. We're on land!"

The others turned to me, and for the first time I noticed that they were quite a bit smaller than I remembered my parents and Rose being.

They took off their helmets to reveal they were all common squirrel monkeys. Their eyes were bright red and evil. The monkeys pointed at me and began to shriek.

Well, I don't know what you do when evil common squirrel monkeys shriek at you, but I would run, so run is what I did. I turned and ran across that wide and bumpy desert, my legs churning in my rubber suit, running so fast that at times it felt as though my feet weren't touching the ground. I ran even though running is my sixth least favorite thing in the world to do, right behind waking up early for school, eating creamed spinach, cleaning my room, getting a haircut, and giving Aunt Dorcas a foot massage.

As I ran across the desert, I noticed a dark shadow slowly begin to fall over me. I looked over my shoulder, expecting to see the three shrieking squirrel monkeys dressed in underwater suits, but what I saw instead was a wave crashing down on me, though it wasn't a wave of water, it was *a wave of squirrels*, a wave of thousands and thousands of confused and wildly screaming squirrels.

And they were about to drown me. I opened my mouth in shock, and as the furry avalanche began to fall, the only thing I could think to scream was—

"Squirrel wave!" I shouted as I suddenly sat up in my bunk, bonking my head on the metal ceiling of the submarine.

"Ow."

I heard three people and one monkey groan.

I was back on the submarine, back in reality. I wasn't in the desert, and I wasn't about to drown in squirrels. Everything was normal, or, at least, what passed for normal with my family. I was alright, or, at least, what passed for alright with me.

"W.B.," Rose moaned from the bunk beneath mine, "one day, you and I are going to have to sit down and figure out where your weird squirrel thing comes from."

"Good luck with that," M muttered into her pillow. "I've been trying to figure it out for years."

Suddenly my father gasped. He popped out of his bunk and rushed over to the steering wheel at the other end of the submarine.

"Sharon! Sharon!" he called. "It's finally here!"

"Mmmmm, that's nice dear," my mother yawned, as she pulled her blanket over her head and tried to drift back to sleep.

"What's finally here?" Rose Blackwood asked as she slid out of her bunk and threw her robe over her shoulders.

"The day is finally here!" my father cried excitedly as he fired up the submarine, making it come to life. The torches mounted to the outsides switched on, the flippers flipped, and the entire metal contraption slowly rose from its slumbering spot at the bottom of the sea. "This is the day we reach the island!"

The thought of finally getting out of the submarine and setting foot on solid land was so exciting that M and I hopped out of our bunks as well, and rushed to the front of the submarine. Together, the four of us did our family happy dance.

For those of you who don't know what that is, it's the dance that my family does when we're really happy about something. It used to be only my mother and father who did the family happy dance, but eventually Rose and I started doing it along with them. I will be the first to admit that our happy dance looks absolutely ridiculous. In fact, it looks insanely ridiculous. When we're doing our happy dance, we sort of look like we're a group of orangutans fighting off a flock of angry seagulls. But I still enjoy doing it. After all, what's the point of dancing if it doesn't make you look a bit foolish?

From his shadowy place in the corner, Waldo stared at us with the sort of look on his face that you'd expect from a monkey watching humans act like apes.

NOBODY GETS TO HIT
W.B. EXCEPT FOR ME

Three hours later, we were there. We had reached the island where Captain Affect and his crew were planning on burying his greatest treasure before his ship had sunk. It had taken us weeks to get there, and we had almost strangled each other on the way. But we had still done it.

"We're here!" P declared proudly, and then he scratched his head. "Now what?"

"I think the first thing we should do is park the submarine and explore the island," said M. "We need to find some supplies. Your greedy monkey ate the last of our food, which means unless we become really good at fishing, we'll need to find something to eat here to survive the trip back home."

Everyone shot an ugly look at little Waldo, who whimpered and frowned.

"I can't believe I made you my first mate," P whispered to the monkey as he shook his head in disgust.

"I thought you didn't *really* make him your first mate," I objected. "You told me you just gave him the hat because his head was cold."

"We both know that was a lie, W.B.," P said as he rolled his eyes. "And stop sticking up for him. You're always defending that naughty monkey."

"What?" I exclaimed, unable to believe my ears. "Me? Defending the monkey? Why on earth would I do that? I've hated that monkey since the beginning of our trip!"

"That's not how I remember it," P said with a sniff, as he picked a flea from his ear.

M steered the underwater ship to the rocky coast of the island, and, once we were as close as we could get, she brought it to the surface and dropped anchor.

We all dressed quickly and climbed out of the submarine, happy to have our first taste of fresh air in quite a long time. We walked across the top of the submarine and hopped onto the rocks jutting out of the side of the island.

"Careful, W.B.," Rose warned, after I'd already slipped and landed face first on a sharp rock. "You don't want to hurt yourself."

"Yeah, thanks."

The island was unlike anything I'd ever seen before. The beaches were covered in pale sand and brightly colored shells. There was a dense, green jungle in the center of the island, where we discovered large fruit bushes which we quickly stripped for supplies. There was a row of coconut trees along the outside of the jungle, and P climbed them with the ease of a common squirrel monkey and picked all of the coconuts clustered at the top. M found several edible plants and nuts and wild tropical vegetables which she'd read about in one of her books. Before we knew it, we had collected a small feast.

As my parents began to lug the bags with food back to the submarine, Rose was hard at work collecting sea grapes and other little edible things along the coast. Once we had enough supplies, we would begin our search for Captain Affect's sunken treasure.

It was my job to find fresh water on the island, which meant I'd need to do a bit of exploring. I took the large clay jugs that my parents had given me and made my way into the jungle in search of a stream or waterfall. As I walked, I heard a rather monkeyish noise behind me, and, the next thing I knew, there was a common squirrel monkey perched on my shoulder like a pirate's parrot.

Waldo smiled at me as though we were now best friends.

"Ooo?" he cooed, in a tone which sounded like he was saying, "Hey, buddy. How ya doing?"

"Go away."

His little monkey lip trembled.

"Stop trembling that lip," I ordered. "I don't care about your monkey tears. You've been horrible to me for weeks, and you even tried to keep P from allowing me back into the submarine. I hate you."

Waldo stopped trembling his lip and bowed his head in shame as he hopped off my shoulder and sat on the ground.

I continued along a path that I discovered, which allowed me to cut through the dense jungle brush with ease. I could hear little Waldo following me, though every time I looked back at him, he'd try to hide behind a bush or a rock or a tree. It was very annoying. Not quite as annoying as Aunt Dorcas, but then again, very few things are.

After what felt like an eternity of searching, I finally found a little pond in the middle of the jungle. Though I can't say that the water looked particularly good. It was dark and murky, with a thick layer of pond scum on top. It also looked like it'd been sneezed in by at least six different wild animals with head colds. As I uncorked the clay jugs to collect the water, I accidentally sneezed in it as well.

I dipped the clay jugs into the water, and as I waited for them to fill, I looked over and spotted someone who had suddenly appeared beside me at the edge of the pond. They were wearing an ugly mask, a pointy witch's hat, and a long, flowing robe. For a moment we just stared at one another.

"Hello," I said.

"Hello," the masked person replied pleasantly.

I looked down and saw that the masked person appeared to be floating two inches above the ground. My brain spun in my head like a cow in a cyclone, trying unsuccessfully to understand what it was that it was seeing.

"I don't suppose you're an illusion?" I asked the masked face. "Maybe you're something that my overactive imagination invented because I'm a little frightened being out here on my own?"

"No," the masked face said. "I don't think so."

"And you're not a bad dream? The sort of dream I'd have after making a grilled cheese sandwich with fried onion rings right before bedtime?"

"Nope. But that sounds delicious."

"It's very delicious. Hmmmm," I said, scratching my chin. "So, you're really here?"

"I'm afraid so," the masked face told me. "I'm really here. And as you might have already guessed, I'm a ghost."

"Oh."

For a moment, my brain broke.

It just sputtered and died, making the noise that a balloon makes when it releases all of its air at once. Everything in my mind shut off after the ghost told me that it was a ghost, so I just sat there staring blankly until my brain somehow fixed itself again.

The ghost was polite enough to wait until my brain was better before it spoke to me again. I will say this for ghosts—they're much more polite than monkeys, eels, and sharks.

I'd never met a ghost before. Then again, I'd never ridden in a submarine before either, or worn an underwater suit, or battled man-eating sea creatures, or made an enemy out of a monkey. So it was turning out to be a summer full of new and horrible experiences.

"A real ghost?" I asked, when I had found my voice again.

"Yes," the ghost said as it straightened out its long, black robes. "A real ghost. And I'm afraid that if you steal the lost treasure of Captain Affect, I'm going to have to haunt you."

Well, that was bad news. If we couldn't take Captain Affect's treasure, then our trip across the Pacific Ocean would have been a remarkable waste of time. Not to mention a waste of all the brain cells I might have killed during my underwater battle—a possible side effect of the hyperventilation, according to M. If I'm going to kill some brain cells, then I at least want a priceless diamond or two for my troubles.

I tried to reason with the ghost.

"What if I took the treasure, but didn't keep it?"

"Hmmm. You mean if you stole it, but then gave it away?" the ghost asked. "Like Robin Hood?"

"Exactly."

Apparently, no one had ever asked the ghost a question like that before, and so it had to think about it for a while. At first I waited politely, but then I began to glance at my pocket watch and repeatedly clear my throat, letting the ghost know that I had better things to do with my time than to sit around and watch it think. If I enjoyed watching others think, I'd randomly walk up to people on the street and say "What's 1,532,263,656 divided by 36,482,468?" or "What number is 'molybdenum' on the Periodic Table of Elements?" or "What does the Swahili phrase '*arobaini na mbili*' mean in English?"

"I don't know," it finally said. "I'll have to ask my fellow ghosts what they think about that. But I have to warn you, I don't think they're going to like the idea."

"Couldn't you try to convince them to like it?"

"Why would I do that?"

"Because we're best friends?" I tried.

"Oh really?" the ghost asked doubtfully. "We're best friends, eh? What's my name, then?"

"Uhhh . . . Mr. Ghost?"

"That's not even close!" the ghost snapped. "Leave that treasure alone, kid, or I'll haunt you. And if you try any funny business, I'll *double* haunt you. And don't ask me what double haunting is. You don't want to know."

He was right. I didn't want to know. To be perfectly honest, I was even more frightened than I was when I was trapped at the bottom of the sea with the shark and the eel.

But once again, I was going to have to pretend to be braver than I actually was. I was getting pretty good at pretending to be brave, though I wished I didn't have to practice it so often.

"I wouldn't haunt me if I were you," I told the ghost.

"Oh really? Why not?" the ghost asked.

I thought for a moment before answering.

"Because I'm a ghost too?"

The ghost reached out and poked me.

"You don't feel like a ghost," the ghost said. "You feel like a regular chubby kid."

I reached out and tried to poke the ghost back, but my finger went right through him. I tried it again, but the same thing happened. I decided to try it one more time, just in case the third time was the charm. Sometimes the third time is the charm. But it wasn't the charm this time. My fingers, hand, and arm all passed through the ghost as though he wasn't there. That upset the ghost. Ghosts are polite, but they really don't like it when you stick your entire arm through them. I don't think I would like it either.

"Oops," I said, as my teeth began to chatter with fear. "Sorry about that, Mr. Ghost. Have I mentioned how much I love your robes? They're very nice and billowy."

"BOOOOO!" the ghost roared, and the next thing I knew, it had shot up into the air, soaring through the sky in a very terrifying and ghostlike way.

I screamed as I turned and ran, nearly tripping over little Waldo on my way down the path.

"Lousy, stupid monkey!" I cried. "Run! Run as fast as your stupid monkey legs can!"

Waldo spotted the ghost in the sky and screamed. He dove further into the jungle and scampered up the first tall tree he saw before jumping to another treetop and then to another, leaping and scurrying while shrieking like a loon.

When you're running away from something frightening, like an angry ghost, sometimes you don't pay attention to where you're going. This was one of those times.

After running as quickly as I could for about fifteen minutes, I realized that I was completely lost. I had left the path I'd originally taken to the pond, and now I was somewhere in the middle of the jungle where the trees were so tall and thick that I could barely see the sky through all of the twisted branches. I heard several different animals cry out, and I hoped that they weren't the sort of animals whose moods would be greatly improved by eating a slow and sweaty kid. I sat on an overturned tree and thought about what I should do next.

I had nothing with me but my clay jugs filled with pond muck. I had left all my other supplies back at the submarine. Suddenly I realized that I was hungry, maybe hungrier than I'd ever been before.

Actually, that's not true. Whenever I'm hungry, I think that it's the hungriest that I've ever been. I'd actually eaten quite recently, and quite a lot too. In fact, my parents and Rose blamed Waldo for eating the rest of our food, but it was actually me who did that. I have a terrible habit of sleepwalking, and sometimes when I sleepwalk, I sleep-cook, and sleep-eat, and then, later on, I sleep-snack on the sleep-leftovers. It's the strangest thing. It sometimes happens while I'm awake too. I'll just be sitting there on the sofa reading, and the next thing I know I have a peanut butter, banana, bacon, and jalapeno sandwich in my hands, with a tall glass of milk and a slice of chocolate cake on the side. And since it's already in my hands, I figure that it would be a shame to waste it, so I'll eat it.

So I guess you could say I felt a little guilty that my parents blamed Waldo for eating all of our food. But only *a little* guilty. That lousy monkey had been picking on me since we found him. And he also got in my father's way when P tried to close the back of the submarine, which meant little Waldo tried to kill me. Sort of.

Although, the more that I thought about it, the more I realized that Waldo probably didn't understand what the control panel was, and how it was being used to save me from the shark and eel. After all, he was only a monkey. He probably hopped onto the control panel for the same reason he hid Rose's hairbrush, picked at the lice in P's hair, and ate all of the bananas and peanuts that M packed. He did those things because he was a monkey. And that's what monkeys do. They don't know any better.

Huh. I supposed I did feel pretty bad for the little guy.

But I didn't have time to feel bad for him for long.

Because as I sat there wondering whether it would be safe to call for help in the middle of the jungle, I heard a bunch of loud screeching noises from up in the trees.

I looked up just in time to see a dozen angry looking monkeys flying towards me. I screamed as I quickly ducked under the fallen tree.

The monkeys landed and immediately began to screech, kicking up dirt and slapping the ground, clearly unhappy that I was trespassing on their land.

"I don't suppose I could convince you all that I'm actually a ghost?" I said to the monkeys.

Judging from the expression on their faces, I could tell that I most likely could not.

"This isn't fair," I told the monkeys. "I've already been attacked by wild animals this week. I should get a free pass here."

The monkeys disagreed, which they did by shrieking and screaming and hurling stones at me. It's strange that I have crazy dreams about squirrels, and yet monkeys were quickly becoming the animal that gave me the most trouble in real life. I really don't know why I don't get along with them better. After all, I love naps and bananas, so you'd think we'd have a lot to talk about.

When they grew tired of shrieking and throwing things

at me, they decided to attack. I'm not much of a fighter, but I still held up my fists as though I knew what to do with them. I'd never hit anyone before, unless you counted all of the times that I'd accidentally hit myself. But I had no choice except to fight. The monkeys were all faster than me, which meant I couldn't do what I normally do, which is bravely run away.

I'd recently decided that I could still consider myself brave if I added the word "bravely" to what I'm doing, even if it might seem cowardly to others. For example: last month, when I found a snake in my boot, I *bravely* shrieked and cried until Rose rushed into my room and took it away.

See? It works really well.

Anyway, back to the monkeys.

The monkeys pounced on me and smacked me upside the head with their strong monkey hands. They pummeled me, kicked me, strangled me, tripped me, bit me, spat in my eyes, and made fun of my haircut. As they beat me, I bravely cried and bravely screamed for help. I bravely begged for mercy as I bravely wet my pants.

I fell to the ground and covered my head and my face, trying to shield myself from all the monkey punches, when suddenly I heard a very familiar sounding monkey shriek.

The monkeys stopped attacking me and started to back away. I looked up and saw little Waldo standing there, waving a stick in the air as he screamed at the other monkeys. The monkeys glanced at each other with confused looks in their eyes, as though they were uncertain if they should be afraid or not. There were many of them, and only one Waldo, but Waldo had *a stick*. A stick! None of them had ever thought to pick up and swing a stick before. It was a brilliant idea, as far as monkey ideas were concerned.

I could see why P had taken a liking to Waldo. He was a very clever monkey. He was a little bit evil, but definitely very clever as well.

"Thanks, Waldo," I said. "I have to say that I was wrong about you. You really are a good monkey."

He quickly spun around and knocked me over the head with the stick.

"Ow! Lousy, double-crossing monkey!"

One of the other monkeys took a step towards me, but, before it could get too close, little Waldo swung his stick at it as well. The other monkeys cowered in fear.

Waldo held up the stick and shrieked as loudly as he could, which caused the rest of the monkeys to turn and run away.

Even though I didn't speak monkey, I knew exactly

what his shriek meant.

"Nobody gets to hit W.B. except for me!"

Does That Mean I Don't Have To Pay You Back The Seven Dollars That I Owe You?

Using Waldo as my guide, I was able to find my way back to the shore where my parents and Rose were waiting.

"Where are the water jugs?" M asked.

I looked at my empty hands and realized that I had dropped the water jugs when the monkeys had attacked me. It was probably for the best. No one should be drinking that sneezy pond water.

"And what's *he* doing with you?" my father asked coldly

as he pointed to Waldo.

"He saved my life," I told P. "There was a gang of angry monkeys who attacked me, and then Waldo appeared out of nowhere and saved me by picking up a stick and swinging it at the other monkeys. It was brilliant. Well, it was *monkey* brilliant, but it was still pretty impressive."

I left out the part about Waldo bonking me on the head with the stick. That wouldn't have made him look very good. Come to think of it, it probably wouldn't have made me look very good either.

My parents and Rose shook their heads slowly, looking strangely doubtful and disappointed, which confused me. I would have thought they'd be happy to hear that I'd been saved from vicious monkeys.

"W.B., you don't need to lie for little Waldo," M said.

Huh?

"Huh?" I said.

"There aren't any vicious monkeys here. I read about this area before our trip so I would know what sort of wild animals to expect. I can understand you feeling upset about your father wanting to get rid of Waldo, but you shouldn't lie to us."

"But I'm not lying!"

"Monkeys don't live in this part of the South Pacific,

W.B.," Rose said. "Mrs. Baron is right. I helped her do her research. There are reptiles and birds here, and a whole lot of bugs, but there are no monkeys."

"Yes there are!" I objected. "They attacked me. Look, I have monkey fist-sized bruises all over my head. Where do you think these came from, huh?"

Rose rolled her eyes.

"W.B. you *always* have bruises on your head. And you also have a really wild imagination. I suppose the next thing you're going to be telling us is that there are *ghosts* on this island as well."

Oh, that's right! The ghost!

With all the monkey madness, I'd nearly forgotten about the ghost.

That shows you just how ridiculous of a day I'd been having.

"But there is a ghost here!" I told her, thinking of what the masked ghost from the pond had said to me. "I saw one while I was collecting water. He told me that he and his ghost friends would haunt me if we stole Captain Affect's treasure. Then he poked me and called me chubby."

"How could a ghost poke you?" P asked. "Wouldn't his finger go right through you?"

"There's no such thing as ghosts, W.B.," M said with

a sigh. "You probably just heard a loud noise or spotted a dark shadow somewhere in the jungle and it frightened you."

When I looked back in the direction of the jungle, I saw not one, but *three* ghosts staring back at me from behind a bush. They all wore the same hideous masks, pointy witch hats, and flowing ghost robes. The one I had met by the pond made a slitting motion across his throat, letting me know that I would be in big trouble if I didn't listen to his warning. Another ghost mimed breaking me in half with his hands. The third one couldn't think of a threatening gesture to make, so he danced a funny little jig instead. Then they all three vanished.

"Leave that treasure alone or I'll haunt you," the ghost had said. *"And if you try any funny business, I'll double haunt you. And don't even ask what double haunting is. You don't want to know."*

"Did anyone just see that?" I said as I pointed to the bushes. "Over there in the bushes?"

M shielded her eyes from the sun as she looked.

"Nope, I don't see anything," she told me. "Maybe you should lie down for a bit, W.B. If you aren't lying to us, then that means you've been seeing things. Maybe you suffered some sort of brain injury when you were underwater.

I warned you about hyperventilation."

"Or maybe you're suffering from a brain injury as a result of all the other times you've hit your head," Rose suggested. "You do hit your head more often than anyone I've ever met. Your poor brain probably just needs a rest."

"There are no ghosts, W.B.," M said. "Trust me. I'm a scientist."

Huh.

I looked back over towards the bushes. Like M and Rose, I now saw nothing. There was no movement or rustling. Just bushes being bushes.

The thought that my brain was playing tricks on me and causing me to see things that weren't actually there was somehow more frightening than any ghost or killer monkey. It meant that I was losing my mind. I didn't have much in life, but I had always had my mind. It wasn't a particularly great mind (I had more than one complaint about it and would exchange it for a better one if I could), but I had no interest in losing it without a fight.

I rubbed my eyes and looked at the bushes again. There was nothing there. I repeated that to myself: *there's nothing there.*

It must have all been in my imagination. It had to have been. M was right. There was no such thing as ghosts. The masked ghost must have lied to me when I asked if he was really there, or if he was just a figment of my imagination. Never trust a ghost to tell you if it's real or not. Apparently they're liars.

I promised myself that I wouldn't allow my mind to trick me anymore. I would outsmart my brain by no longer listening to it. If my brain told me that I was seeing a ghost, I would simply tell my brain that it was wrong. It was wrong because it was impossible, just like the killer island monkeys. And I only believed in possible things.

Suddenly, I felt very embarrassed for making a fool of myself in front of Rose and my parents.

"You're right," I quickly told M. "I was lying about the ghosts and also about the killer monkeys. I know they don't exist. I guess I'm just in a lying mood. But don't worry. I'm not losing my mind. I'm just a liar. Hey, P, your hair looks very nice today."

"Really?" said P with a smile, as he gently patted his porcupine hair. "Thank you for noticing, W.B. It has been much pointier lately."

"W.B., stop lying to your father and follow us, please," M said, as she and Rose climbed into the submarine. "We'll collect more water after we've found the treasure."

"Actually, I've just thought of a way to filter the salt

from the sea water so we can drink it," my father chimed, pulling his pen and paper from his pocket and jotting down some scientific notes.

Waldo and I started walking back to the submarine, but before little Waldo could get too far, P turned around and pointed at him.

"Not so fast, *monkey*," P said with a frown. "You're going to stay here while we search for the treasure. I haven't decided what we're going to do with you yet."

My father climbed back into the submarine, scratching his itchy head as he slid down the hatch.

M flipped a switch and cranked a dial on the control panel, and suddenly the torches attached to the sides of the submarine began to glow twice as bright. In an instant we were able to see everything in the dark waters surrounding the island. There were brightly colored fish and coral, as well as a forest of slimy looking seaweed.

"Everyone, keep your eyes open for any sign of a shipwreck," said M.

P steered the submarine around the island, moving

slowly to ensure that we wouldn't miss anything or hit any of the sharp-looking rocks that jutted out from the ground like claws. P and M stared out the large front window of the submarine, while I looked through the eyeball shaped windows on the left, and Rose looked through the eyeball shaped windows on the right.

As we searched, P began to tell us how difficult it would be to actually find Captain Affect's ship.

"I want you all to understand that finding a ship-wreck in the sea can be a lot like finding a needle in a hay-stack," he said, scratching his chin and neck as he steered. "Though why you'd be so careless as to leave one of your needles in one of your haystacks is a mystery to me. I always make it a point to keep my needles and my hay-stacks very far apart, thank you very much."

It was true. He did. If you want to make my father angry, you need to do one of three things: Be rude to one of his pets. Make fun of his hats. Or place one of his nee-dles near one of his haystacks.

"Anyway," P continued, scratching the inside of his ears. "It's going to be very difficult to find the ship. It might take us days to find it, maybe even weeks. We might be search-ing for months before we—"

"There it is," Rose said as she spotted the old shipwreck.

"Right," said P. "That is a sunken ship. But we don't know if that's the ship that we're looking for. It might not be the ship that belonged to Captain Affect. It could have belonged to anyone. We don't know—"

"It's his ship," I interrupted. "It says so on the side of it. See? 'Captain Affect's Ship.'"

It's certainly not the most creative name for a ship that I'd ever heard, but I suppose it got its point across.

"Errr . . . right," P said as he began to circle the shipwreck. "But you should all understand that there is a chance that the treasure might not be there. Someone might have already taken it, or it might be buried beneath the ocean floor, or maybe it was never there to begin with. We shouldn't de—"

"Nope," M interrupted. "There it is. I see the treasure. Right there."

M pointed to a large treasure chest on the deck of the shipwreck, right across from where the mast had snapped in half. The treasure was sitting there, out in the open, just waiting for someone to take it. It almost seemed too easy. All that we had to do was go and get it. And by "we," they meant "me."

"Would you mind, son?" P asked sheepishly as he pointed out the window.

"I mean, if it's not too much trouble?" added M. "And try to breathe normally this time."

I sighed.

"Just give me the stupid rubber suit."

P handed me the underwater suit. He had glued the crack in the helmet and replaced the air hose, so it was almost as good as new. He told me that it should be fine as long as the glue didn't get too wet.

"Ready, W.B.?" Rose asked.

"Ready as I'll ever be."

M pulled me aside and whispered to me.

"Are you sure your mind is alright, W.B.? I'm still worried about you."

"My mind is as good as it's ever been," I assured my mother.

For some reason, that didn't appear to make her feel any better.

After I slipped the underwater suit and helmet back on, M opened the back of the submarine, and I stepped out onto the ocean floor. This time, I wasn't as frightened as I was before. I was actually excited to collect the treasure, which Vice President Levi P. Morton would use to save the country. I'd be a hero, a national hero, and for a reward, my family would be presented with the Wish Diamond, a diamond so beautiful and enchanting that I was actually tempted to steal the picture of it from the Vice President's book.

I slowly made my way to the shipwreck and climbed onto the deck. Though the sails had disintegrated, the cannons had rusted, the mast had snapped in two, and most of the wood had splintered and rotted, I could still imagine how impressive Captain Affect's ship must have been several hundred years ago. It was incredible to be standing on a part of history that most people thought had disappeared forever.

Using every ounce of might I could muster, I reached down and carefully lifted Captain Affect's lost treasure chest. It was much heavier than I thought it would be, but my excitement had given me twice my usual strength.

As I held the treasure in my hands, I felt something pass through my mind that I can only describe as a warm sort of tickle, as though someone had poured hot tea into my ears and added a squirt of honey.

I assumed it was the feeling of pure joy.

Standing there on the deck of the sunken pirate ship, with a literal fortune in my arms, I took a moment to appreciate the silent beauty around me. There were many people in the world who would have given anything to be where I was, so that they could learn the secrets of what went on at the bottom of the sea. I felt like the luckiest person on the planet.

And then I spotted something out of the corner of my eye which was either a sea monster or a giant collection of seaweed floating towards me. When I had finished bravely screaming, I decided that I had appreciated the ocean for long enough and quickly made my way back to the submarine.

P used his tools to break down the old and rusty locks that fastened the treasure chest shut. While he did that, M took a rag and wiped the sea gunk off the chest, revealing the name "CAPTAIN AFFECT," which had been carved into the chest with a chisel. There were also several carvings of skulls and crossbones under the name, which, I suppose, were meant to frighten away people who tried to steal the treasure. Or maybe the captain was simply practicing his artwork. Either way, they were very nice and pirate-ish, which made the treasure seem very authentic.

After P had removed the lock, he placed his hands on the corners of the chest and prepared to open it.

"Is everybody ready?" he asked.

"Yes!" we all cried.

"Are you sure?"

"Yes!" we all cried again.

"Are you positive?"

"Yes!!!"

"Are you surely positive?"

"McLaron," my mother said with a forced smile, "just open it."

"Right."

My father opened the chest, revealing a treasure which no one had seen in hundreds of years.

It was the most beautiful thing imaginable.

No. It was even more beautiful than that.

Have you seen pictures of pirate treasurers? This was 4,578 ½ times better than that because it was real and because it was right there in front of us. There were shiny coins, and glittering rubies and emeralds and sapphires, pearl and diamond necklaces, and bracelets, crowns and tiaras, golden swords, silver daggers, and so much more. It lit up the inside of the submarine with a rich and vibrant glow.

We dropped to our knees with our mouths wide open because it was so overwhelming. Several minutes later (when we were all nice and normally whelmed), we jumped up and began to celebrate, whooping like maniacs as we did the happiest happy dance imaginable. We danced every dance we could think of, including "the stinky onion," which we danced until my head somehow got stuck in the stove.

The fun always stops when my head gets stuck in the stove.

Then we dove into the treasure chest, trying on the crowns and necklaces and rings, tossing the gold coins into the air and letting them rain down over us. We dug through the treasure as though we were greedy pirates ourselves, pulling out bejeweled cups, and diamond encrusted pins, silver plates and golden mirrors, feeling richer and more successful than we'd ever felt before.

After we spilled the rest of the treasure onto the floor of the submarine, we found the prized jewel of the loot, the piece of the treasure that had been promised to us by the Vice President of the United States as a reward: the Wish Diamond.

My mother picked up the giant diamond with hands that shook with awe. The diamond shimmered brightly in the torchlight of the submarine. It was a perfect shade of light blue and reminded me of the glaciers that we had seen in the frozen arctic when my family traveled around the world in our Air Oh! Plane. It was the most stunning object that my eyes had ever had the pleasure of eyeballing.

In fact, it was the most stunning object that *any* of our eyes had ever eyeballed, and, because of that, we couldn't look away from it. We just sat there on the floor and stared at the grapefruit sized diamond, the huge diamond that would make us the richest inventor family in the country, maybe even the world.

When our eyes began to grow sore from staring at the Wish Diamond, M and P started up the submarine, and we began our journey back to the California coast. The trip home would be long, but we didn't care. We had our beautiful diamond to keep us company, our one-of-a-kind diamond which would make us rich enough to have the life that we had always wanted. And not only would we be wealthy, we would also be national heroes. Maybe Vice President Morton would give me another medal to place beside my WORLD'S GREATEST GRANDMA medal. Maybe one that says I'm also the world's greatest grandpa.

I was so distracted that I didn't realize we'd forgotten a former furry passenger of ours back on the island: the common squirrel monkey that had saved my life.

I also didn't realize that there were three new passengers on the submarine, passengers who only I could see.

I first spotted the new passengers a few days later, when I was waking up from a nap in my bunk. I opened my eyes and saw three floating ghosts, ghosts who couldn't possibly be there because my scientist mother had told me that ghosts don't exist.

"Hello," one of them said to me in a friendly voice. "I warned you about taking the treasure. Remember? Now we're going to have to haunt you. And because you weren't honest with your parents, and you didn't give them our warning, we're going to *double* haunt you."

"You aren't going to haunt me or double haunt me or even triple haunt me," I whispered back, "because you aren't real. There's no such thing as ghosts."

Then I closed my eyes and turned over, pulling my blanket over my head. Before I fell back asleep, I heard one of the ghosts whisper to another.

"Wait, if we aren't real, does that mean I don't have to pay you back the seven dollars that I owe you?"

A Very
Weasely-Looking Face

The trip back home felt shorter than the trip to the island, but that was mostly because everyone was in such a great mood because of the treasure. We were at sea for almost a week before I realized that we had forgotten little Waldo.

"We aren't turning back for a monkey," P told me after I had mentioned it to him. "And living on that island will be great for him anyway. There's plenty of fruits and nuts for him to eat, and plenty of tall trees for him to climb. He'll be happy there. Probably."

"Though he will be pretty lonely," one of the ghosts added. "The killer monkeys who live there aren't very friendly. And the ghosts who used to live on the island are no longer there to keep him company."

"I don't think that's correct," another one of the ghosts said to him.

"What do you mean?"

"You said that the ghosts who used to *live* on the island are no longer there."

"Yeah. So?"

"Ghosts aren't alive," the ghost pointed out. "They can't be *living* on the island if they aren't alive."

"Oh. Good point. But it would sound really strange to say that there were ghosts *deading* on the island, wouldn't it?"

"I suppose. Perhaps we could say that the ghosts were *ghosting* on the island."

"Oooh, I like that. *Ghosting.* Good word. Well done."

"Thank you. I thought of it while I was *ghosting* earlier this morning."

"Ghosting."

"*Ghosting.*"

I kept telling myself that the ghosts weren't there, and that my brain was wrong, and that I couldn't be seeing what I was seeing or hearing what I was hearing. I was clearly suffering a brain injury from one of the 6,548 times that I'd accidentally hit my head, and the best thing for me to do would be to ignore the impossible and pay attention to the possible. Instead of focusing on the ghosts who weren't there, I focused on my final pirate book instead, though I can't say that I was enjoying the story very much. It was about a ghost that haunted an old sunken treasure, and, quite frankly, I was a little tired of the subject.

"That's a great story," one of the ghosts told me as he tapped my book with his see-through ghost hand. "I know the ghost from it quite well. He's an old buddy of mine. His name is Frank. Good guy. Cooks a delicious meatloaf."

I told myself that the ghosts would disappear once we left the submarine, once my brain had finally had enough time to heal from the terrible injuries that had scrambled it like an omelet. I would start thinking clearly again, and everything would go back to the way it was before.

But several days later, when we arrived at the California coast, the ghosts were still there with me. The three of them sat beside me as the Air Oh! Plane took off and headed towards Pitchfork. They took turns licking their ghost fingers and sticking them in my ears, but I kept ignoring them. They were just a part of my wild and stupid imagination.

Sometimes I really hated my wild and stupid imagination.

Especially when it got the inside of my ears wet with ghost spit.

We arrived at the Baron Estate later that morning, and found a very annoyed looking Aunt Dorcas sitting in her rocking chair on the front porch. She glared at us as we stepped out of the winged flying machine, which P then shrunk with his Shrinking Invention. She clearly hadn't forgiven us for abandoning her for over a month without telling her where we were going.

Again.

We tend to abandon her a lot.

"What is that thing?" she asked, as she pointed to the treasure chest that Rose Blackwood and I lugged inside.

We had promised Vice President Morton that we wouldn't tell anyone about the treasure, and that included Aunt Dorcas.

"It's nothing," M told her.

"Nothing at all," P agreed.

"Yup, it's nothing," Rose said.

"What treasure chest?" I asked, as the four of us went

inside.

It was wonderful to be home again. I had missed the Baron Estate terribly. It was dry, safe, quiet, boring, and totally free of sharks and eels. I walked across the familiar living room, up the familiar steps, and down the familiar hallway, until I reached my favorite place in the world: my familiar bedroom. It was just as I had left it.

. . . With the exception of my three new roommates.

"Sheesh, you've got a lot of books, kid," one of the ghosts told me as he stared at my bookshelf.

"Do you happen to have a spare bed that I can sleep in?" another asked. "I have a bad back, and I can't really sleep on the floor."

"It smells oddly like cheese and stale pie in here. But other than that, it's a pretty nice place," the third ghost said. "I'm really going to enjoy haunting this room for the next sixty or seventy years."

It's a good thing that those ghosts weren't really there. Otherwise, I might have been a bit frightened.

The Vice President had told us to wait at the Baron

Estate after we returned with the treasure and that he'd be in touch with us shortly. So we waited and we waited. And then we waited some more. And then some more. And then some more. And some more.

"Maybe we should write to Vice President Morton?" P suggested one morning, when we were all sick and tired of waiting.

"He told us that he would contact us, McLaron," M said. "Remember? We're just supposed to wait here and guard the treasure. I don't want to disobey an order from the Vice President of the United States."

It made us nervous, having all that treasure in the house. It was literally a fortune—the biggest fortune that anyone in Arizona Territory had ever seen. Because of that, my parents didn't feel safe leaving the house. They were convinced that if they left for even an hour, then someone would break into the Baron Estate and steal the treasure. Which of course, meant that they would steal our Wish Diamond as well—after all, there was a very good reason why that diamond was the most stolen diamond in history. It was so beautiful that *I* often wanted to steal it, even though I was technically one of its owners. It just had that special *stealy* quality to it.

M and P didn't want Rose and me to leave the house

either, in case we accidentally told someone about the treasure, someone who might be tempted to come over to see it in person. They didn't even feel comfortable letting Aunt Dorcas leave the Baron Estate, which my aunt found quite confusing, because she didn't even know about the treasure.

"Why can't I leave the house?" she asked my mother. "I'm supposed to meet my best friend Madge Tweetie in town for tea. If I don't show up, she'll say all sorts of foul things about me to the other ladies. She's *always* looking for opportunities to say foul things about me to the other ladies. Madge, that stinker . . ."

"I can't tell you why," M said. "Please just trust me, Dorcas."

I guess you could say that we all ended up growing pretty paranoid. We thought we heard noises at night, noises that sounded like someone prowling around outside of the Baron Estate. We began to wonder if perhaps someone was spying on us. Suddenly, my parents didn't feel comfortable having everyone go to sleep at the same time, just in case someone broke into the Baron Estate and stole the treasure while we were all asleep in bed. M and P decided that we should trade off staying up all night, keeping watch over the treasure to make sure there was an eye on it at all times.

The first night, my father stayed awake and guarded the treasure. And then the next night, my mother stayed awake, and then Rose Blackwood had a turn, and then the following night my father said that he would stay awake with the treasure again.

"What about me?" I asked. "I haven't had a turn yet. I can guard the treasure if you like."

Rose, M, and P all looked at each other with doubtful expressions on their faces.

"Well, W.B.," Rose finally said, "we *would* give you a turn. But you've been acting really funny lately."

I didn't know what she meant.

"I don't know what you mean."

"W.B.," my mother said gently, "you've been talking to yourself a lot lately, which is fine. There's nothing wrong with that. Your father and I sometimes talk to ourselves when we're deep in thought. But lately, you've been arguing with yourself as well, and telling yourself that you aren't going to listen to yourself because you aren't really there. You tell yourself that you're imaginary, scientifically impossible, and that you aren't going to allow your damaged brain to trick you. And also that you should keep your ghost spit to yourself. It's really quite weird."

"It's very weird," my father said. "So we think you should rest for a while until your brain is better. Or at least less weird."

"My brain is fine," I argued, and then, before I could stop myself, I shouted, "and the three of you need to stop making faces at me!"

M, P, and Rose stared at me in shock.

The three ghosts, who were invisible to everyone but me, were standing behind my parents. They were sticking their tongues out at me.

"We're not making faces at you," M said slowly.

"This is just what my face looks like," P said as he pointed to his face. "I can't help it if it looks a bit funny."

"Maybe you should lie down, W.B.," Rose Blackwood said as she gently took me by the arm. "Get some rest. Then you'll see that no one here is making faces at you."

"I was!" one of the ghosts called out. "I was making faces at you! See?"

And then he made an awful face at me.

I shook off Rose's hand, my cheeks burning crimson in embarrassment.

I needed to prove to my family that I wasn't losing my mind. Perhaps if *they* truly believed that my brain was healthy, then *I* would start believing it as well, and then I'd no longer be haunted by ghosts that weren't there because *ghosts do not exist.*

"I'm fine," I insisted. "Please let me guard the treasure tonight. I deserve a chance. After all, I'm the one who actually went into the sea and got it. I'm the one who battled a shark and a giant eel. You wouldn't even have a treasure to guard if it weren't for me. I'm perfectly healthy. My mind is fine. In fact, it's better than fine."

"Then why do you keep arguing with yourself?" M asked.

That was an excellent question. What excuse could a healthy kid have for regularly arguing with himself and telling himself that he doesn't really exist?

"I have an imaginary friend!" I finally declared. "And it's perfectly normal for a kid to have an imaginary friend that he talks to."

My parents and Rose thought about this for a moment, before nodding their heads.

"He's right," M said. "That is perfectly normal. I had an imaginary friend growing up too."

"I had lots of imaginary friends," Rose admitted. "In fact, when I was little, *all* of my friends were imaginary."

"I had an imaginary flying dog named Fred-Head," P said. "But we aren't on speaking terms anymore."

"Why not?" I asked.

My father's expression turned very sour.

"Fred-Head *knows* what he did."

And that's all that he would say on the subject.

That night, I finally had my turn to stand guard over the treasure while everyone else slept. I was happy to help the family and prove to them (and myself) that I wasn't losing my mind. I didn't have a scientific brain, but it could be counted on to stay awake and pay attention when necessary. My brain could at least manage that much.

Or so I thought.

I suppose it was kind of scary sitting there in the dark living room, listening to the cold and howling desert winds outside as they beat against the walls and windows of the Baron Estate. And I probably would have been frightened if I was alone.

But of course, I had my three "friends" there to keep me company.

When I was certain that everyone in the house had fallen asleep, I decided to speak to the ghosts. They might have been imaginary, but I was getting bored, and an imaginary conversation would be better than no conversation at all.

"So, were you all pirates back when you were still alive?" I asked.

The ghosts were so happy that I was finally paying attention to them that they forget they were supposed to be haunting me. They answered me proudly, one at a time.

"Nope. I was a butcher."

"I was a baker."

"I was an accountant."

"What's an accountant?" I asked.

"Don't ask," the other two ghosts said quickly as they shuddered, not wanting to listen to the third ghost talk about his boring former job.

"Okay. So if you weren't pirates, then why are you haunting a pirate treasure?"

The three ghosts looked at each other and frowned. Or at least, I *assumed* that they were frowning. It was hard to tell what was happening behind their ugly masks.

"Back when we were still alive, each of us tried to find the treasure of Captain Affect," one of the ghosts said as he sat down beside me. "I grew tired of being a poor baker, so one day I sold my shop, bought a ship, and went off in search of the treasure. Being a treasure hunter seemed like a much better job than a baker. At the very least, I'd get fewer crumbs down my trousers. I'd heard stories about how magnificent the treasure was, and that it was just sitting there in the sea, waiting for someone to claim it. It seemed like an easy way to get rich quick."

"What happened?" I asked.

The ghost suddenly looked really embarrassed.

"When I got to the island, I accidentally ate a poisonous mushroom and died," he admitted. "In fact, all three of us had deadly accidents when we reached the island."

"I was hit on the head by a falling coconut while I was eating my lunch," another ghost said. "I fell face forward into my lentil soup and drowned. Otherwise, the soup was pretty good."

"I went swimming in the ocean right after eating, without waiting for a half hour first," the third ghost told me as he rubbed his belly. "There's a reason parents tell you not to do that."

I was amazed. The ghosts seemed even clumsier than me. I'd been through a lot, but I'd yet to drown in soup.

"Then why were you haunting the island?" I asked. "How did you become ghosts?"

The three ghosts leaned in towards me.

"Have you ever heard of a *pirate's curse?*" one of them whispered.

"No."

"Well, there's a thing called a *pirate's curse*. You see, when a pirate dies while trying to hide his treasure, that treasure gets hit with a pirate curse. It's the most powerful curse known to man."

"That's the most ridiculous thing I've ever heard," I said.

Apparently, that was a very offensive thing to say. The three ghosts took turns lifting me up and dropping me from the ceiling until I apologized for calling the curse ridiculous.

"Since we died on that island while searching for the treasure, we were all hit by the pirate's curse," one of the ghosts said. "So now we're doomed to haunt anyone who steals the treasure."

"Wow," I said, as I thought about the poor ghosts' fate. "That's awful. Did you know about the curse of Captain Affect's treasure when you decided to quit your jobs and search for it?"

"Yes," a ghost admitted, "but it sounded like the most ridiculous thing I'd ever heard."

The other two ghosts then took turns lifting *that* ghost up and dropping him from the ceiling until he apologized for calling it ridiculous too. Really, he should have known better. A pirate's curse is nothing to laugh at.

"So what can break the curse?" I asked.

All three ghosts tilted their pointy heads as though they hadn't understood me.

"Huh?" they all said at once. "What do you mean?"

"I mean, I've read enough adventure books to know that no curse lasts forever. There has to be something that can stop the curse and allow you to move on."

"Move on? What do you mean? Move on to where?"

one of the ghosts asked.

I shrugged.

"I don't know. Where would you like to move on to? I can't imagine you want to spend the rest of eternity haunting an old treasure you weren't able to steal."

The ghost thought for a moment, stroking the bottom of his mask like it was his chin.

"I've always wanted to go to Cleveland," he finally said.

"Cleveland? You mean Cleveland, Ohio?" I asked with a frown. "Okay, I'm not sure you understand what I mean by *move on.*"

But the other two ghosts agreed with him. They'd always wanted to see Cleveland as well. That's where they wanted to go, and I couldn't convince them of anything else. Not that I tried particularly hard. I had enough on my mind without worrying about how a trio of goofy ghosts would choose to spend all of eternity.

"Alright," I said. "We need to do what we can to break the curse, so the three of you can finally move on . . . to Cleveland."

If I were them, I'd want to move on to the afterlife. But if they wanted to go to Cleveland, then I would do my best to send them to Cleveland.

At this point, you might be wondering if I actually believed that the ghosts were there, or if I believed that they were simply a part of my wild and crazy imagination.

Well, I'll tell you.

I don't know.

So there you are.

Alright?

Good. Glad we cleared that up. Now, back to the story.

"Where did you learn about breaking curses?" one of the ghosts asked.

I told the ghosts to follow me, and the four of us headed upstairs to my bedroom. We went through my bookshelves, and I picked out all of my adventure books where the hero had to break a terrible curse. I sat on the floor and showed the ghosts the different ways to break curses, by defeating an evil villain, or kissing an enchanted princess, or destroying a haunted amulet, or saying a magical phrase. None of those seemed particularly helpful for our situation (though one of the ghosts repeatedly suggested that he should kiss Rose Blackwood, just to be certain), and it all seemed rather hopeless until I found a book about a curse placed on a treasure by an evil pirate king.

I suppose that book probably should have been the first one I looked at. After all, it was called *The Pirate's Cursed Treasure*.

The hero was able to reverse the pirate's curse by returning the treasure to its original owner. That allowed the ghosts who were haunting him to finally move on to the afterlife.

"Yes!" cried one of the ghosts when I explained it to them. "That makes perfect sense! If you return the stolen treasure to its original owner, I think we can finally move on to Cleveland!"

"There's just one small problem . . ." the ghost who used to be an accountant pointed out politely.

But the other two ghosts and I weren't interested in hearing about that one small problem, no matter how politely he brought it up. So we ignored him.

"This is a bit awkward," I said, "but my family and I originally went hunting for this treasure because the Vice President of the United States asked us to. He said that it would help save the country from bankruptcy."

"Did he also say to keep it a secret?" a ghost asked.

"Yes."

The three ghosts shook their heads at me in a disapproving manner. They were right. I shouldn't have told them about Vice President Morton. I'm terrible at keeping secrets, especially ones regarding national security.

"So you can see what a difficult situation I'm in," I told them. "If I return the treasure to its original owner, it would set you free to go to Cleveland, but it would be devastating to the country, and it would break a promise to the Vice President. And if I give the treasure to the Vice President and save the country, then you three won't be able to move on, and you'll haunt me forever."

"We're actually not haunting you," one of them explained. "We're *double* haunting you. When a ghost double haunts you, they make it so no one else can see them *except for you*. That way, when you try to tell people that you're seeing ghosts, they'll think you're lying, or crazy, or both. And eventually you'll start to think you're crazy as well. It really is the best way to haunt someone."

"Ohhhh. That's pretty clever."

"Thank you," one of the ghosts said with a proud grin. "But don't worry. We won't do it forever. Just for the rest of your natural life. After that, you'll become a ghost like us.

That's how it works."

I can't say that I liked that idea very much. I mean, there were clearly some good things about being a ghost. I would never again trip and bump my head because I'd be able to float and travel through walls. But if I were a ghost, I'd never be able to eat another sandwich or slice of pie, which was a very depressing thought. There was also the matter of ghost clothing, which I can't say that I particularly enjoyed.

"When I'm a ghost, will I have to wear an ugly mask and pointy witch hat like you?" I asked.

The three ghosts looked hurt as they removed their masks and hats, revealing perfectly ordinary faces underneath. I was expecting them to look ghostly and horrific, but they simply looked like see-through versions of boring people you'd see on the street. The one who used to be an accountant looked particularly boring.

"You think these are ugly?" the butcher ghost asked.

"I thought they looked fun and *ghosty*," the baker ghost said with a frown.

"I spent two days making these," the accountant ghost muttered.

After I apologized and told the ghosts that the masks and the hats were indeed quite fun and ghosty, we made our way back to the living room. I tiptoed down the stairs while the ghosts floated two inches over them, which, frankly, made them look like showoffs.

I promised the ghosts that I would speak to my parents and Rose the following morning. I knew they would never believe that the treasure was actually haunted, but I also knew that I might be able to convince them to return it to its rightful owner. My parents believed that there was nothing more important than doing the right thing, even if it meant missing out on wealth and riches beyond imagination. My mother once told me that there was never a good excuse for stealing, and *technically* we were stealing the stolen treasure. Even if we were stealing it in order to save the country, it still didn't belong to us. I knew that if I put it that way, they'd have to understand.

But when the ghosts and I got back to the living room, we made a terrible discovery.

Captain Affect's treasure was gone.

I searched the entire living room, but it was nowhere to be found.

"Ahem, excuse me? Remember that *one little problem* that I mentioned earlier?" the accountant ghost said as I searched. "That one little problem that none of you wanted to hear about? When we were upstairs, I saw someone sneak into the Baron Estate, and then sneak out with the treasure. See? This is what you get for not listening to me."

My jaw dropped in shock. The other two ghosts' jaws dropped as well. We stood there for a moment with our jaws dangling like slobber on a fat dog's tongue before I was hit with a thought that gave me hope.

"Wait a minute. Does that mean you three will now go and haunt that person? The person who stole the treasure from my family? Am I finally free?"

The three ghosts shook their heads.

"Nope. You're still stuck with us. The curse forces us to haunt the person who stole the treasure from the shipwreck, not the person who stole the treasure *from* the person who stole the treasure from the shipwreck. You'll get to haunt him when you become a ghost. And don't worry, we can teach you how."

As generous as their offer was, I didn't really feel like haunting anyone. I felt like curling up in bed and never getting out again. I had let down my family. I had let down the ghosts. I had let down the Vice President of the United States and the entire country. And I'm sure there were even more people who I'd let down that I couldn't think of at the moment.

"Did you get a good look at the person who stole the

treasure?" I asked hopefully.

"Yes," said the ghost, "but I don't think it'll be very much help to you. I don't know his name, and I didn't see where he was going. I just saw that he had a very weasely-looking face."

DOUBLE DORCASED

"Weasel Face took the entire treasure?" Rose Blackwood repeated in disbelief. "He didn't even leave us the Wish Diamond?"

"It's true. He took the whole thing," one of the ghosts told her.

I nodded my head but then remembered that Rose couldn't see or hear the ghosts.

"That's right," I said. "And then he left without saying a word."

"That's very strange," M said as she removed her glasses and wiped them with her handkerchief. "Why would he wait until the middle of the night to collect the treasure? And why would he break into our home to take it? We were going to hand it over once Vice President Morton sent for us. This is very odd."

"Do you think he took it without Vice President Morton knowing about it?" Rose asked. "Maybe he got greedy and decided to steal it all for himself. I knew we shouldn't trust that weasely-faced man."

"That's right," P agreed. "You should never trust anyone who looks like a weasel. You should only trust people who look like trustworthy animals, like owls or penguins or giraffes."

"Why are giraffes trustworthy animals?" I asked.

P rolled his eyes and then looked at me as though I was the world's biggest dolt.

"When has a giraffe ever lied to anyone?"

He was right. I couldn't think of a single instance.

"We can't just sit around and let him get away with it!" Rose argued. "We went through a lot to find that treasure!"

"She's right!" one of the ghosts exclaimed. "Come on, everyone! Let's go get that treasure!"

The other two ghosts and I stood up to follow him, but then I once again remembered that no one else could see them. I wished the ghosts hadn't decided to *double* haunt me. It made things very awkward and embarrassing.

"What do you suggest we do?" M asked. "We don't know where Vice President Morton's office is. They blindfolded us for the ride there, remember?"

"I honestly don't know if there's anything we *can* do," P admitted. "We can't just board the Air Oh! Plane and fly around looking for a white building with tall columns out front. That would take ages."

"You're right," Rose said miserably. "I guess your inventions can't help us this time."

"Maybe they can," one of the ghosts muttered out of the corner of his mouth.

I looked at the ghost and raised an eyebrow, as if to say, "What do you mean?"

The ghost shrugged, as if to say, "I mean what I mean."

I raised my other eyebrow, as if to say, "Yes, but your meaning wasn't very clear."

Another ghost coughed into his fist, as if to say, "I'm coughing into my fist."

I wiggled both eyebrows at him, as if to say, "Quiet, you. We're trying to have a silent conversation here."

"I happened to notice that your father has a new invention in the pocket of his coat," the shrugging ghost said to me as he continued to shrug. "Maybe that new invention can help?"

"P, are you sure that you don't have something that can help us?" I asked him. "Maybe you have something useful that you're keeping in your coat pocket."

P reached into his coat pocket and pulled out a Swiss cheese sandwich with extra tomato.

"You're right, W.B.," he said as he began to eat the sandwich. "Maybe eating this sandwich will give me the strength to think up an idea."

"Other pocket," the ghost whispered to me.

"Other pocket," I told my father.

After P finished his sandwich, he reached into his other pocket and pulled out a little invention which looked a bit like a mechanical pickle.

"Ohhhh," he said, as he whacked himself on the forehead. "That's right! I had forgotten about this!"

"What is it?" Rose Blackwood asked.

Instead of simply answering, P pressed a little green button on the side of the invention before rushing outside.

We all grabbed our coats and followed him, with the three ghosts floating right on our heels.

"Would you mind not floating right on our heels?" I whispered to one of the ghosts as I tripped over my feet while attempting *not* to trip over his nonexistent ghost feet, and fell into the dirt. "I just washed my face, and I'd prefer not to get dirt on it."

"Sorry. Sheesh, you're clumsy, kid. I didn't think it was

possible for a ghost to trip someone. We don't even have real feet. I'll bet you sometimes trip over your own shadow, don't you?"

"No, I don't," I lied. "Now hush."

P had stopped beside our white picket fence, and we all lined up behind him. We stood in front of the Baron Estate as the morning sun rose over the sloping sand dunes of the Pitchfork Desert, shrinking the shadows and bathing everything in gold. It was usually warm in Arizona Territory, but I could tell that today was going to be uncomfortably hot.

The six of us (three people and three ghosts) watched as P held one end of his mystery invention up to his eye, while pressing the little buttons that ran across the length of the device. It sort of looked like he was playing a clarinet, but, instead of putting one end to his mouth, he put it to his eye.

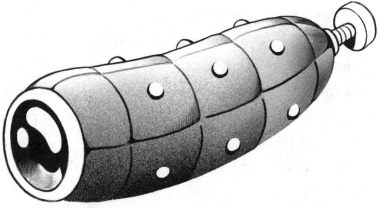

So I suppose it was nothing like playing a clarinet. Sorry. I was just trying to find a good comparison. I guess there isn't one.

"McLaron, what is that thing?" my mother asked.

"Hah!" P said as he lowered the invention.

There was a black circle painted around his eye.

"It's a device that I invented a few months ago, and I forgot to tell you all about it," P said with an excited gleam in his blackened eye. "When we were traveling around the world in the Air Oh! Plane, I was a tad bit worried that we might misplace our map and get lost. So I invented something that would record where we had gone, the entire route we traveled, and it would show us how to get back home again."

"Fascinating," M said.

"Interesting," Rose commented.

"Defenestrating," I added.

Alright, I didn't know what that word meant. And I didn't really understand my father's invention and how it could help us. But everyone else had said something, and I felt left out.

"I accidentally left the invention on," P continued, "and it's recorded every place we've gone over the past few months. If you look through the picture end of the invention, you can see the route we traveled to get to the island. And if you go a bit further back, you can see the route we traveled to get to Vice President Levi Morton's office. We now know how to get there!"

That was fantastic news! We were so excited that we started to do our family happy dance, spinning around and slapping our hands against our knees, when I noticed out of the corner of my eye that the ghosts were staring at us strangely.

"Are you alright?" one of them asked with a frown. "You look as though you're being attacked by your own underpants."

My father used to have a horse named Magnus, but he gave that horse to a friend of mine who had helped us defeat Benedict Blackwood. So now we're horseless. Having no horse would make travel difficult for some people, but not for my family. P's oldest and most reliable invention is his horseless carriage. It's a large buggy with two rows of comfy leather seats, and four wooden wheels with metal rims. It has a lever to control the speed, and a little handlebar to control the direction. There's a metal crank at the front of the carriage that you have to wind up every hour or so in order to make the carriage go. The carriage makes a terribly loud noise as it travels down the road, but it gets you from Point A to Point B pretty quickly, unless of course you accidentally wind the crank too much, in which case you'll end up at Point R, or in some horrible cases, Point Ψ. But if you know what you're doing, there are very few better ways to travel.

We all packed overnight bags (just in case), and quickly boarded the horseless carriage. As M began to wind up the crank at the front of the carriage, my eggy Aunt Dorcas suddenly came rushing out of the Baron Estate.

"Wait!" she screamed. "Wait! Don't leave me alone again!"

Her face was still bright purple from her bad experience with the Gravity-Switcher-Ma-Thinger. It was beginning to look as though her face would be that color permanently. She'd tried covering it up with powder, but, when she'd sweat beneath the desert sun, her true purple color would shine through.

"There's no time to wait, Purple Dorcas!" P declared as he slipped on his driving gloves, driving cap, driving goggles, driving shoes, and driving nose plugs. "We're on a mission to save the country!"

"But we can't tell you anything else about it," Rose added. 'Sorry. Top secret."

"There's egg salad in the ice box for you to eat if you get hungry!" M called.

Aunt Dorcas looked as though she was going to explode. Her purple face turned a deep and dark color that I can only describe as *zorple*. Her angry little hands formed angry little fists, and then she began to run as quickly as she could.

I have to say, she moved much faster than you'd expect a person of her size and shape to be able to move. In fact, she looked a bit like an eggy bolt of lightning, jumping over the white picket fence with a single leap, and dashing across the dunes with the grace and agility of a pregnant cheetah.

Never underestimate an angry Dorcas.

P pressed the lever to direct the horseless carriage forward, but before the buggy could move an inch, my zorple faced aunt dove into the air and landed in the seat between me and Rose Blackwood.

"I'm coming with you," she said through gritted teeth. "Accept it."

"But Aunt Dorcas," Rose began, "we made a promise

to—"

Aunt Dorcas shot Rose a look so angry and severe that it made the sister of the most dangerous man in the world close her mouth in an instant.

"Alright," M said slowly. "I guess Dorcas will be joining us."

Aunt Dorcas smiled brightly, excited to finally be a part of one of our adventures.

I suppose it was a bit unfair for us to leave her at home alone all the time. After all, she was a part of the family. Even if it *was* the annoying part.

As my mother adjusted the speed of the carriage and steered, P held his invention up to his eye in order to see the path that we had traveled to Vice President Morton's office.

"What do you call that invention, Mr. Baron?" Rose Blackwood asked.

"Good question, Rose. I call it my *G.P.S.* Device."

"What does G.P.S. stand for?" M asked. "Global Positioning System?"

"Of course not, that would be a silly name," P said with a chuckle. "It stands for *Going Places, Stephen?*"

"...Oh."

"Where are we going?" Aunt Dorcas asked as she settled into her seat. "How long will it take to get there? Will we be stopping for lunch? Did someone pack a lunch or will we be eating in a restaurant? If we eat at a restaurant, they better serve soup. I want soup. The soup better not be too salty though. Soup is so salty nowadays. It makes my tongue itch. Does anyone have a blanket? I'm cold. But I'm also a bit thirsty. Is there any water? Any cold water? What about a handkerchief? May I use someone's handkerchief? I would use mine, but it's too pretty, and I don't want to use it to blow my nose. The sun is really bright today. Does anyone have an umbrella? Or sunglasses? The sun is bothering my eyes. And I can already tell that it's giving me a sunburn. Does it look like my skin is burnt? I'm probably as red as a lobster's behind. Do I look like a lobster's behind? Waldo, please scoot over. I need to put my feet up. In fact, Rose, would you please scoot over as well? I'd like to lie down. Sharon, I'm going to take your coat and use it as a pillow. Oh, this is an uncomfortable coat. It's so itchy! Does anyone have a more comfortable and less itchy coat that I can use as a pillow? Sharon, stop driving over those big bumps. The bumps are upsetting my stomach and giving me a headache. Drive slower, please. Slower! Oh no. I have to use the bathroom. You're going to have to drive me back to the Baron Estate because I refuse to use a public bathroom, and I *absolutely* won't be using a public outhouse. The thought of using a public outhouse is enough to give me an even more upset stomach. And it's making my eye twitch. I need my eye medicine. *Why is this coat so itchy???*"

My mother obeyed, turning the horseless carriage around and driving back to the Baron Estate while Aunt Dorcas continued to complain about everything and anything. Rose and I found little pieces of inventor's putty which we jammed into our ears with the hopes that it would block out my aunt's voice. Unfortunately, it didn't work. Aunt Dorcas was just too good of a complainer.

We pulled up to the white picket fence of the Baron Estate. As my aunt left the carriage and disappeared through the front door of our home, my father and mother silently nodded to one another, before winding the carriage and driving away as quickly as they could.

"Oh my goodness," said one of the ghosts who'd been sitting behind me. "I would gladly suffer through a hundred thousand pirate curses if it meant I never had to spend another moment with that woman."

"I know," another ghost said as he clutched his head. "I didn't know a person could complain that much. I still have her voice echoing in my skull."

I leaned back and whispered to the ghosts in a low voice.

"See, this is why your *double* haunting didn't bother me that much. I've spent my entire life being double Dor-cased."

AREN'T THEY PRETTY?

We continued to follow the route that P had recorded in his G.P.S. Device, which led us all the way across Arizona Territory and into New Mexico Territory. We'd been blindfolded during our original carriage ride with Knuckles and Mongo, but the familiar smells and sounds let us know that we were headed in the right direction.

The horseless carriage traveled through several small towns along the New Mexico Territory border, and it received the same strange looks that my parents' inventions tend to get when seen by people who aren't familiar with wacky inventors. Several cowboys and farmers and ranchers stared slack-jawed at the puttering horseless carriage, with its leather seats and mechanical engine, but the biggest reaction to the invention came from their horses. The horses all

turned up their long noses and made "Hmmmphhh!" sounds of annoyance at the brass and wood buggy which basically did their job for them. I suppose I would react the same way if I came downstairs for breakfast one morning and found a mechanical son sitting in my place. Knowing my parents, that's a definite possibility.

After we passed through several smaller New Mexico Territory towns filled with more slack-jawed ranchers and annoyed horses, we found ourselves riding up a long and empty road. Aside from the clockwork chugging of the horseless carriage and the soft whisper of the winds, it was dead quiet. It seemed as though there wasn't another living creature within ten miles.

"Are you sure this is the right way, McLaron?" M asked.

P lowered the G.P.S. Device from his face. It had once

again left a thick black ring around his eye. The black ring looked a bit like shoe polish.

"Of course I'm sure. Has the G.P.S. Device ever been wrong before?"

"I don't know. We've never used it before."

"Good point," my father admitted. "But I trust this device, just as I trust all of my inventions. I swear on my life that if I build something, it will be built to last."

Suddenly the horseless carriage began to sputter. And it wasn't the good kind of sputtering. It was the kind of sputtering that let you know that there was a problem, a serious problem that was about to get a whole lot worse. The carriage made more loud noises as the wheels began to slow, and soon the invention came to a complete stop. A thick cloud of smoke began to pour out from underneath the buggy.

My parents got out of their seats and went to the front of the carriage, where they proceeded to turn the crank over and over again. But the winding did nothing but exercise their arms. The buggy would not move. My father opened the front panel of the carriage and waved away the black smoke, before leaning forward and staring at the clockwork parts which normally worked together in perfect harmony to make the invention move.

"Hmmm . . ." P said, as he stared at the clockwork parts while stroking his chin, "I think I know what's wrong with it."

"You do?" I said hopefully.

"Yes. It's broken."

Unfortunately, we didn't have any tools or materials that my parents could use to fix the horseless carriage, which meant there was only one thing left for us to do.

"I guess we give up," I said as I lay down on the side of the road. "I think I'll take a nap. Wake me up if another carriage comes by to save us. Otherwise, I'll just lie here and wait to become a ghost."

"Good plan," said one of the ghosts, and he and his ghost buddies joined me on the ground.

"Not so fast," M said as she pulled me to my feet. "We aren't giving up. And for the last time, W.B., there is no such thing as ghosts."

"Yeah, W.B.," said one of the ghosts as he gave me a shove. "There's no such thing as ghosts."

"I suppose we should start walking," Rose Blackwood said with a frown, as she lowered her hat brim to shield her eyes from the sun. "Lead the way, Mr. Baron."

My father held the Going Places, Stephen? Device to his eye, and pointed us further east. We had no choice but to follow.

Walking in the desert at the height of the summer afternoon's heat was just as miserable as it sounds. After an hour, we were all covered in sweat, and our tongues hung from the corners of our mouths like old shriveled socks. The long and empty road appeared to go on and on with no town or building or even a single tree in sight. There was no water, no shade, and we were beginning to lose hope.

Even the ghosts were miserable in the heat. They kept muttering to each other about how they should have never left their tropical island to follow a chubby fool like me into the desert. I couldn't help but agree with them. I wished I was relaxing on a tropical island as well. I wouldn't even mind the killer monkeys.

"Are we close?" M choked, as a hot desert wind sent a spray of sand into our faces.

"Close to what?" P asked as he lowered the G.P.S. Device.

There was another thick, black ring around his other

eye.

"P, did you know that every time you hold that thing up to your eye, it leaves a black ring?" I asked.

"Yes," P told me with a devilish giggle. "You know I have a wicked sense of humor, W.B. I coated the eyepiece of the G.P.S. Device in shoe polish. What a great gag! Hahaha!"

"But you're the only one whose eye keeps getting blackened," Rose pointed out, as she mopped her forehead with her red bandana.

P shrugged. "It's still funny."

The three ghosts collapsed on a sand dune by the side of the road. They looked terrible, even for ghosts. They had removed their masks, caps, and flowing ghost robes, and were wearing three of the silliest looking bathing suits I'd ever seen. I pointed and laughed but then got a mouthful of sand when a desert wind blew in my face.

"Serves you right," one of the ghosts muttered bitterly. "This is awful. I hate the desert. I've got sand in my ear."

"I've got sand in my nose."

"I've got sand in . . . *other* places."

"P, can't you think of an invention to help us?" I wheezed. "Maybe you could invent us some sort of flying machine out of . . ." I looked around the desert to see what he could use as building material. ". . . I don't know. Sand?"

P shook his head as he wiped the sweat from his face, smearing the black shoe polish into his spiky white hair.

"I'm sorry, W.B.," he said. "There is nothing that we can do but walk. Come on, everyone. The G.P.S. Device says we're almost there."

Eventually, the sun slowly began to set, which was nice for a few moments, but then the cold night winds started to blow, and suddenly we were all freezing. The ghosts regretted leaving their masks and hats and robes behind, and their teeth chattered loudly as they rubbed their bare arms for warmth.

We heard the howl of coyotes, followed by the screech of a predatory bird, and then the unusually loud yawn of a tortoise.

Our path grew dimmer, and the shadows cast by the night soon drowned the lumpy sand dunes in blackness as the last ray of the sun disappeared. The light provided by P's G.P.S. Device began to flicker, and soon he was barely able to see the little line that showed him where to go.

We stumbled and shivered almost blindly until I cleverly tripped over something which we quickly realized was the front step to a large white building with tall columns.

"We're here!" Rose said through her chattering teeth.

Since we were all too cold to do any sort of proper happy dance, we sort of waved our hands and hummed happily instead.

"This is proof that we can do anything we set our minds to," M said as we all huddled together and hugged. "I am very proud of each and every one of you. This is truly a—"

"What's that smell?" Rose interrupted.

"I have no idea," said P as he made a sour face. "Phew, it stinks!"

"Please don't interrupt me when I'm trying to . . ." M began, but then she trailed off and covered her nose with her hands. "Oh, my goodness! You're right, it smells awful!"

I smelled it too. We looked around, trying to see what it was that smelled so badly, and then Rose had the idea that we should all check the bottoms of our shoes. M, P, and Rose's shoes were all clean. So were the three ghosts', who checked the bottoms of their ghost shoes just to be certain. That left only my shoes.

I lifted my left shoe and saw nothing underneath it.

"It's not me," I told everyone. "I'm clean."

"Check your right shoe," Rose said.

I checked my right shoe.

Oh.

Apparently, someone in the area had forgotten to clean up after their dog.

The last thing I wanted to do was show up to the Vice President of the United States' office with dog poo on my shoe. So, while my parents and Rose waited, I rushed around to the side of the building and found a broken ice box that was being used as a dumpster. I opened it and found stacks of old newspapers, some of which were ten or fifteen years old. I tore out one of the pages from a newspaper from 1881. I was about to wipe the gross bottom of my shoe with it, when I happened to spot something very interesting printed on the page.

It was very interesting indeed, as well as very confusing, very educational, and very frightening.

"Did you clean the mess from your shoe?" one of the ghosts asked as I rejoined my family at the front steps of the white building.

I nodded yes to him, and then held my index finger to my lips, letting him know that he and the other ghosts should be quiet. And perhaps because the ghosts were so tired from the long walk across the desert, they actually obeyed me.

We entered the building with my father leading the way. There were no men in long black coats waiting out front like before, but, once we were inside, we could see that the lobby and the hallway were brightly lit, which meant that someone was there.

We walked quietly through the narrow hall. The pictures and paintings, which had been flipped over the last time we were there, were now turned over so we could see them properly. They were all pictures and paintings of very smug and slimy looking people who were posing in front of various treasures and large stacks of money. We kept walking until we came to the door that Mongo and Knuckles had knocked on before.

"Look," M whispered. "The American flag is gone."

She was right. The flag that had been tacked to the door was no longer there.

"Maybe it's in the wash?" P suggested. "It might have gotten dirty from all the people knocking on it with their filthy knuckles."

He leaned forward, and, after wiping his filthy knuckles with his handkerchief, he knocked on the door.

From inside, we could hear the sound of papers shuffling, drawers closing, gold coins jingling, jewels clacking, and finally the sound of a treasure chest being pushed slowly under a desk.

"What's the password?" someone from behind the door called.

"Weasel face," said my father.

We heard someone inside grumble about how stupid it was to keep the same password all the time, but then the door slowly opened.

It was Weasel Face, and beside him were Knuckles and Mongo. They didn't look particularly happy to see us, especially not Weasel Face, who probably couldn't have looked happy even if he tried.

"Yes?" said Weasel Face in his funny little accent. "What can we do for you?"

"Our son says he saw you break into our home and steal Captain Affect's treasure," P said. "Is that true?"

"No," Weasel Face said quickly.

P smiled and shook Weasel Face's hand warmly.

"Oh, well, alright then. Sorry to disturb you. Have a great evening, boys."

My father turned to leave, but M quickly caught him by his collar.

"You didn't steal the treasure?" she asked Weasel Face, squinting sharply at him until her face began to look a bit weasely as well. "Are you being honest with us? We walked a long way to get here, and we deserve to know the truth. Are you *sure?*"

"Of course I'm sure!" he snapped. "Please don't insult my intelligence. I wouldn't forget stealing a treasure from someone. I didn't do it. You have my word as a Veezlefayce, which is the most honorable promise that can be made. Now, if you like, I can arrange for a carriage to take you back to your home."

"We don't have any money with us," Rose Blackwood told him. "We can't afford to pay for a carriage ride all the way back to Arizona Territory."

"That's okay," said Knuckles as he rose to his feet. "We can lend you some money."

"Yeah," Mongo said. "We'll just give you a couple of gold coins from the treasure we have hidden under this desk."

Knuckles pulled Captain Affect's treasure chest out from behind the desk and opened it, taking a few coins and offering them to Rose.

Veezlefayce looked at Mongo and Knuckles as though they'd just blown their noses on his mother's best Sunday dress.

"Oh . . ." said Knuckles after a moment, understanding what they'd just done.

"Oops," said Mongo, "I mean . . . what treasure?"

With his weasel face burning bright red, Veezlefayce turned back to my parents.

"I suppose you think I should be embarrassed," he said quickly. "Well, I'm not. I wasn't *technically* lying. I didn't *steal* the treasure from you. You were going to give it to us anyway, remember? I can't steal what's being given to me. I just took it without telling you. There's a big difference."

"That's true," P agreed. "After all, we found that treasure so we could bring it here to save the country from going bankrupt."

"But they were supposed to leave us the Wish Diamond," Rose objected. "It was promised to us by Vice President Morton. It's ours."

Veezlefayce's weasel face looked so furious, that for a moment I was worried he was accidentally going to swallow his own chin.

"Fine," he finally said through gritted teeth. "You shall have your precious little Wish Diamond."

He dug through the treasure chest, pushing aside gleaming gems and shining coins and golden crowns until he found the most impressive part of the treasure: the Wish Diamond. As he held up the diamond, it caught the light in the office and twinkled like the night's brightest star. Mongo and Knuckles stared at it dumbly with their lower lips drooping like codfish, though to be fair, they usually stared at everything dumbly with their lower lips drooping like codfish.

I could see from the look in Weasel Face's eye that he didn't want to hand over the diamond. While the rest of the treasure would be enough to purchase a small country, that diamond was, by far, the most impressive part of Captain Affect's loot. As I stared at it from across the room, I had the sudden urge to steal it, despite the fact that it was being given to my family. Something about that diamond seemed to whisper, "Steal me! Do it! I'm yours! I'm alllllll yours, W.B.! Use me to buy alllllll the sandwiches that your belly desires! With extra pickles. I know how much you love pickles. Aren't you hungry right now? You look as though you haven't eaten in ages . . ."

"I *haven't* eaten in ages," I whispered to the diamond.

"What? You just ate a few slices of cheese two minutes ago in the hallway," one of the ghosts said to me. "And you ate at least three dozen caramels while we were walking through the desert, even though one of the worst times to eat caramels has to be when you're walking through the desert. That's why you kept choking."

The ghost gave me a little shove. I looked away from the diamond and rubbed my eyes.

Had the Wish Diamond actually been hypnotizing me?

As Veezlefayce was about to hand the diamond to my parents, he was suddenly interrupted by the sound of a very important man clearing his throat from the other side of the room.

You can always tell when it's an important man who's clearing his throat, because it sounds something like "Hummmbullarumpphhrumpphhrumphhff."

"Hummmbullarumpphhrumpphhrumphhff."

Out of the shadows appeared the man who had asked us to go on the treasure hunt to save the country.

"What a pleasure it is to see you again, Baron family,"

Vice President Morton said with a smile so sugary and sweet, that it actually smelled like fresh caramel (or maybe that was just my breath from my desert dessert). "I'm so glad you found your way here. Although I must ask . . . how *did* you find your way here? And also, Mr. Baron, why do you have two black eyes?"

"The answers are actually related," said P, as he wiped the black shoe polish from his face. "Remind me to tell you about them some other time, Vice President Morton, sir. Now, you'll be giving us our reward for finding the treasure, correct?"

Levi Morton's smile flickered as he walked over to us. He took very slow and deliberate steps.

"Reward?" he asked with a mischievous sparkle in his eye. "Whatever do you mean, *reward?*"

"The Wish Diamond," M answered. "You told us if we found Captain Affect's treasure, you would allow us to keep the diamond as a reward, remember?"

The Vice President pretended to think for a moment, as though he was searching deeply through his memories for that promise. As a person who often pretends to think (it's much easier than *actually* thinking), I'm always able to spot a fellow fake thinker. We tend to look up, tap our chins, scrunch our brows, and "hmmmm" a lot more than real thinkers do.

"Hmmm, no," he said as he tapped his chin. "I don't recall that. In fact, that doesn't sound like something that I would say at all. You must be mistaken."

My parents and Rose reacted as though they'd just been punched in the gut.

"But . . ." M began in a weak voice.

"You said . . ." Rose said through quivering breaths.

"I got shoe polish in my eye . . ." P said, but he said it in a devastated sort of way.

Levi Morton walked over to Veezlefayce and took the Wish Diamond from him. He dropped it back into the chest with the rest of the treasure and closed the lid.

"I'm sorry, Barons," he told us. "But you will not be getting the Wish Diamond. I will, however, give you something more valuable than any jewel or treasure. I will give you the sincere thanks of the second most important person in the country, the thanks of the Vice President of the United States."

"Great," I said. "When will we finally have the chance to meet him?"

The man who had been claiming to be Vice President Levi P. Morton froze in place, his eyes as wide as a pair of Aunt Dorcas's apple pies. He started to speak and then stopped, as though his mouth had suddenly forgotten how to form words. Mongo and Knuckles looked at him sympathetically. They knew the feeling. They often forgot how to form words.

My parents looked stunned by my comment as well. Rose raised an eyebrow in curiosity.

"I don't understand," the man claiming to be Levi Morton finally said when he could speak again. "What do you mean? You've already met him. Him is me. I am him. I am Vice President Levi P. Morton."

I took a brave step forward.

"No, you aren't," I told him, reaching into my pockets. "And I can prove it."

From my right pocket, I pulled out the folded up page from the old newspaper I had found outside.

"Here is the proof that you are a liar and a thief!"

And then from my left pocket, I pulled several little stones that I'd taken from the bottom of the sea. They were smooth and brightly-colored and would look wonderful in the candy dish that he kept on his desk.

"And here are the replacement decorative rocks that I promised you," I added. "I hope you like them. Aren't they pretty?"

A HAIRY LITTLE COWBOY

After the man who claimed to be the Vice President thanked me for the decorative rocks, he tried to grab the newspaper away from me. But I was too fast for him. I pulled it away and handed it to my mother, who unfolded the page.

"Oh," she said in a mildly surprised tone. "It's a picture of Levi P. Morton driving the first nail into the toe of the Statue of Liberty."

She looked up at the fake Vice President and frowned.

"You look completely different than you do in this picture."

"That picture was taken ten years ago!" the fake Vice President argued. "I bet you all looked a lot different ten years ago. People change."

He was right. I looked very different ten years ago. I was mostly bald, could barely speak, and went around in diapers (I was a baby, in case you couldn't figure that out). But that wasn't why I was surprised by the article. And it wasn't why I now knew that the man claiming to be Vice President Morton was a fake.

"I'm aware that people's appearances can change after ten years," I said to the fake Vice President. "That's not what I found suspicious. What I found suspicious was what you said the last time we were here, when you explained to us the reasons why this country was out of money."

"What do you mean?" the fake Vice President asked, his face growing pale.

I began to pace—explanations often seem a lot better and cleverer if you pace. Try it, if you don't believe me. But be sure to pace slowly. If you pace quickly while you explain things, people will either think that you're a lunatic, or that you really need to use the bathroom. Also, try not to hyperventilate while you do it. It might seem like you're helping your brain by giving it extra oxygen, but you're actually not. I don't know the exact reason why, but it has something to do with science.

"You mentioned that the government wasted a lot

of money *buying a big copper statue*," I began, "and *the big copper statue* you were referring to was obviously the Statue of Liberty."

"Yes," the fake Vice President said. "So what?"

"But the United States of America didn't *buy* the Statue of Liberty. It was a gift from France. They paid for the shipping as well. And the cost to put up the statue in New York was covered by over 100,000 donations, many of which came from generous, private citizens of the United States, which you would have known if you were *really* Vice President Levi P. Morton! Because in 1881, Levi P. Morton was the Ambassador to France! He knew all about it! He drove the first nail into the statue's big toe! That's what this newspaper article is about. And the fact that you didn't know that *proves* that you are not the Vice President!"

I want you to take a moment to think about what I just said, and how I figured that all out.

Why should you take a moment, you ask?

Because I'm one hundred percent certain that I'll never

be that clever again.

"He ain't the Vice President? I'm confused," Mongo said to Knuckles. "Are you confused?"

"No," Knuckles replied. "But then again, I haven't been paying attention."

"You're an impostor!" P cried as he pointed at the fake Vice President. "I can't believe we used our inventions to help you! I bet you weren't even going to use this treasure to save the country, were you? How dare you lie to us, Mr. Morton!"

The fake Vice President rolled his eyes as he removed his fake mustache, mussed up his hair, untied his tie, and unbuttoned his fake collar. Suddenly he looked much more comfortable, and much less important.

"Of course I'm not going to use the treasure to save the country," he said with an ugly scowl. "And my name isn't Mr. Morton. It's James Reavis. I'm a professional criminal, not a politician."

"What?" P gasped, turning to Veezlefayce. "Can you believe it, Weasel Face? His name isn't actually Levi

Morton!"

"Of course I believe it!" Veezlefayce snapped. "I knew all along, you chowderhead! I'm partners with him. I'm a criminal too. And my name is not Weasel Face. It's Veezlefayce! Veezlefayce!!! It means kidney bean! Knuckles! Mongo! Tie up the Baron family! Do not let them escape!"

Before we could move, the two shaved gorillas grabbed us and tied us to the cushioned chairs in the office. The chairs were really quite soft. I was scared, but at least I was comfortable.

"You just *had* to come snooping around here, didn't you?" James Reavis snarled. "You couldn't leave well enough alone, could you, Barons? The treasure of Captain Affect is mine, and nothing will stop me from having it!"

"We have been looking for it for ages," Veezlefayce told us as he stood beside James Reavis. "We sailed to the island and searched the surrounding waters, but we found nothing. We did everything we could to find the treasure. We even tried to train monkeys to dive into the ocean to search for us, but the monkeys hated the water and ended up turning evil. Well, actually, they turned *more* evil. Monkeys are pretty evil to begin with. Lousy, evil monkeys."

"Do those evil monkeys now live on the island?" I asked, giving a long look towards my mother, who had repeatedly told me that there were *no* monkeys there.

"I suppose. We abandoned them when they disobeyed us," Veezlefayce said as he reached into the desk and pulled out a pistol.

"I told you I wasn't lying," I said to M.

"I'm sorry I doubted you," my mother told me. "But now is not the time for saying I-told-you-so, W.B."

"Sorry, M."

"We tried to hire some professional treasure hunters to help us," Veezlefayce said, as James Reavis pulled out a pistol and pointed it at us as well. "But they all refused. They were afraid of the curse of Captain Affect, which is absolutely ridiculous."

"Ridiculous," said one of the ghosts with a smirk.

"Preposterous," said a second ghost.

"Ludicrous," said the third.

"Ambidextrous," I added.

Alright, I didn't know what that word meant either. But once again, I wanted to add a single word just like everyone else.

"Huh? You're ambidextrous?" James Reavis asked as he frowned at me, before shrugging off my comment. "After my partner and I read about your family's brilliant inventions, we knew that you would be the perfect people to help us find the treasure."

"But we knew that you might need a bit of convincing," Veezlefayce added. "We couldn't let you know that we were criminals. We had to pretend to be trustworthy and important people, so James pretended to be Vice President Levi Morton."

"I made my own Vice President costume," James Reavis chimed.

"It was very nice," my father said approvingly.

"We disguised our secret hideout to look like a respectable office that might be used by the Vice President. Our plan was simple. We would convince you that your country needed your help, and that you would be rewarded with a beautiful diamond if you found the treasure. But when you came back from the island, we would just steal the treasure from you and give you nothing. This, as you can see, is precisely what we did."

"That's evil," my mother whispered.

James Reavis and Veezlefayce turned to each other and grinned.

"Yes," James said, "it was pretty evil. Well done, Veezlefayce."

"Thank you. You did a good job too, James. This has been one of our better crimes."

They shook hands. They were pretty proud of themselves. I suppose they had a good reason to be proud. It was a great plan. I wished that I had a great plan, or any sort of plan. I would have even settled for a slightly rotten one.

"What are you planning on doing with us?" I asked.

The two evil men stopped shaking hands as they considered my question.

"Hmmm, good question. What *should* we do with the Barons?" Veezlefayce asked.

"Well, clearly we can't let them leave here," James Reavis said. "That means they'll need to be *taken care* of. Let's leave it up to Knuckles and Mongo. They're very good at *taking care* of things. Knuckles and Mongo, how do you think you should *take care* of the Barons?"

Knuckles and Mongo looked like a pair of dogs who'd just heard someone set down their supper dishes. They weren't particularly great at "discussing things" or "listening to others" or "sitting in their chairs without drooling," but they were wonderful at taking care of things. Especially if taking care of things meant they were allowed to use their giant fists to beat us senseless.

"We could pummel their bodies until they look like pudding," Knuckles suggested as he cracked his knuckles.

"Or maybe bash their faces into jam," Mongo replied.

"I've already had jam today," Knuckles argued. "I'm in the mood for pudding."

"I don't like pudding," Mongo dismissed. "It's too creamy."

"You could compromise by crushing our bones into jelly," I told them.

"Or beating our faces into a custard," added P.

"Or mashing our toes into potatoes," M said.

"Or whipping our brains into cream," said Rose.

"No," I told her. "Mongo doesn't like things that are too creamy."

"He's right," said Mongo. "And thank you for listening."

Knuckles and Mongo sat on the sofa and continued to discuss their options. They took their beatings very seriously, especially the way they described them.

"Well, I don't care what Mongo and Knuckles do to you, or how they describe it," James Reavis said as he grabbed one handle of the treasure chest. "They can fry your kneecaps into pork chops for all I care, as long as you're unable to ever tell anyone about the treasure. I'm getting out of here. So long, suckers!"

Veezlefayce grabbed the handle on the other end of the treasure chest.

"That's right!" Veezlefayce cackled wildly. "So long,

suckers!"

The two villains each took a step in the opposite direction, trying to pull the treasure chest along with them. They looked at each other and frowned.

"What are you doing?" Veezlefayce asked James.

"I was about to ask you the same thing," James said to Veezlefayce.

"I'm taking the treasure back to my home country, where I can live like a king," Veezlefayce told him.

"No, you're not. Because I'm taking the treasure to Cleveland, where *I* can live like a king," James responded.

"Ah, Cleveland," one of the ghosts said with a sigh. "Maybe one day we'll get there . . ."

"Can't you guys help me?" I whispered to the ghosts. "I know you're cursed, and you need to keep double haunting me, but if you ever want to be free, you're going to need to get me out of here so I can return the treasure and break the curse."

The three ghosts thought about that for a moment. They gathered together in a little ghost circle and had a little ghost discussion about what they should do. As the ghosts discussed whether or not they would help me, Veezlefayce and James continued to pull on opposite ends of the treasure chest, growing more and more annoyed with one another.

"I'm in charge here," James Reavis argued. "I'm the Vice President!"

"You only got to pose as the Vice President because you have that silly American accent!" Veezlefayce shot back.

"It's not silly! What's silly is your name, Weasel Face!"

"It's Veezlefayce!!" Veezlefayce screamed so loudly that his face turned bright zorple. "Veezlefayce! Why is that so hard for you all to understand???"

Finally, the ghost circle broke up, and the three of them floated over to me. I looked up at them expectantly.

"Well?" I whispered.

"W.B., who do you keep whispering to?" P whispered to me. "I really worry about you sometimes."

"I'm whispering to your old imaginary dog, Fred-Head. And you should know that he's very angry with you."

My father turned whiter than the ghosts who were floating beside me. A lump formed in his throat.

"Fred-Head is angry?" he asked nervously. "What did he say? Why is he angry with me? What did I do?"

"He said that *you know* what you did," I replied before turning back to the ghosts.

"We've decided," one of the ghosts began, "that we cannot do anything to stop them. We cannot stand in the way of destiny. That's not what ghosts are supposed to do. I'm sorry."

"What?" I said, my brow crinkling in anger. "What do you mean?"

"What we mean is that we cannot untie you," another ghost continued. "And we also can't do anything to the two villains with guns."

"*It means kidney bean!* It's a normal name in my country! It's as normal as Smith, or Brown, or Jackson is in this country! *Veezlefayce*!!!!!!"

"We also can't do anything to the large men who are planning on hurting you," the third ghost said, as he gestured to Mongo and Knuckles.

"Maybe we could chop them like a salad?" Knuckles suggested. "My wife told me that I don't eat enough greens."

"I hate salad," Mongo said with a frown. "Maybe we could squish them like grapes?"

"So you're useless," I muttered to the ghosts. "Great. Thanks for nothing. Now you'll never get to Cleveland."

The three ghosts smiled. I didn't know what they had to smile about. Their lives (or deaths, or ghostings, or whatever they wanted to call their existence) were just as bad as mine, if not worse.

"But we *can* tell you one thing," said one of the ghosts.

"Oh yeah? What's that?"

"Tell Fred-Head I'm sorry for everything that happened," P whispered to me. "I was young and stupid. I had no idea that a goat would get that upset if you dressed it in a petticoat. I shouldn't have blamed Fred-Head for the fire in the barn or for what happened to the old man whose boots exploded."

One of the ghosts whispered to me.

"Scoot your chair back, W.B."

For a moment, I sat there quietly and waited for the ghost to explain what he meant. I felt certain that one of them would take the time to tell me why and how I would be saving myself and my family simply by scooting my chair back. But the ghosts continued to silently float and smile, refusing to provide me with any more of an explanation. They probably enjoyed being so vague and mysterious. Lousy, stupid, vague, and mysterious ghosts . . .

I sighed. Scoot my chair back. Why not? I didn't have a plan. I might as well listen to the ghosts who were probably just a part of my wacky imagination anyway. At least then I'd be trying something instead of nothing. I'd been trying nothing for quite some time, and it didn't appear to be helping.

Even though my hands were tied behind my back, I was still able to scoot my chair all the way back until I had reached the eastern wall of the office. My parents and Rose Blackwood watched me quizzically as I scooted, and after a moment, they all scooted back as well.

"What are you doing?" M whispered to me.

"Ten," whispered one of the ghosts.

"Just wait," I whispered back to my mother.

"This treasure is going to Cleveland!" James Reavis yelled at Veezlefayce. "End of argument!"

"Wrong!" Veezlefayce yelled back. "This treasure is going to my home country, end of argument times twenty!"

"Nine," whispered another ghost.

"Maybe we could knead them like dough?" Mongo asked.

Knuckles burped into his knuckles and then rubbed his tummy.

"I've been eating too much bread lately," he said. "It's been making me feel bloated. Maybe we can shred them like carrots?"

"Eight," whispered the third ghost.

Veezlefayce and James finally dropped the treasure chest and pointed their pistols at one another.

"I will shoot you if I have to!" James told his former

partner. "I won't even feel bad about it!"

"Seven."

"I won't feel bad about it either!" Veezlefayce sneered. "In fact, I'll enjoy it! I'm a very dangerous man!"

"Six," hissed two of the ghosts at the same time.

I began to hear a deep rumbling sound. At first I thought it was coming from my stomach. I was quite hungry. I noticed James Reavis's candy dish on his desk. It looked like he had jelly beans. I love jelly beans.

"Five."

The rumbling sound grew louder, and soon I could actually feel the rumbling under my feet. The pictures on the office walls began to vibrate. The lamp began to shake. The entire building was buzzing.

Oh, that's right. Those aren't jelly beans.

"Maybe we could mush them into porridge?" suggested Knuckles.

But why must they look so tasty?

"Four."

Veezlefayce and James put their fingers on the triggers of their weapons.

"How many people have you shot?" Veezlefayce asked his former partner.

"Five hundred," James Reavis said through gritted teeth

as he aimed his pistol. "That makes me much more dangerous than you."

The rumbling continued to increase, both in sound and intensity. The office walls began to crack. A beam from the ceiling split and dropped to the floor, missing Rose Blackwood by only a few inches.

"Three."

"Hah!" Veezlefayce cried triumphantly. "I've actually shot five hundred *and one* people! I win! I'm more dangerous than you! The treasure is mine!"

"How about we churn them like butter?" Mongo said to Knuckles. "You can put butter on almost anything."

"Two," the three ghosts said together, before they slowly disappeared.

"Only one of us will get out of here alive with the treasure!" James Reavis spat at Veezlefayce. "Only one!"

"One," I said.

As everyone stopped arguing and turned to me, the floorboards in the center of the room suddenly ripped apart as though they were being pulled by a giant pair of invisible hands. They cracked and splintered into sawdust, as the walls that made up the lovely office began to crumble. James and Veezlefayce screamed as they dropped their guns and backed away from the treasure chest, terrified by the catastrophic earthquake which was threatening to swallow the entire building.

Have you ever been sitting there and watching as something amazing was about to happen, knowing for certain that what you were about to see would be the most incredible thing you've ever witnessed? But then, when it actually happens, it's far more amazing, ridiculous, impossible, incredible, and *weird* than you could have ever dreamed?

Well, this was one of those times.

The ground opened up and little Waldo emerged, riding on the back of a giant earthworm.

See? I told you so.

It was the earthworm that P had accidentally *biggened* back at the Baron Estate, the one that had burrowed deep into the ground before we had the chance to shrink it again. It must have found its way to an island the South Pacific, where it was befriended by a common squirrel monkey named Waldo.

Little Waldo shrieked loudly as he rode the giant earthworm, shaking his stick in the air as the worm flopped down and crushed Mongo, Knuckles, James Reavis, and Veezlefayce, dragging the four of them into the tunnel which led to the other end of the world. The common squirrel monkey shrieked his goodbye to us as he and the giant worm followed the evil men down the tunnel where they disappeared for good, leaving me, my parents, and Rose Blackwood staring dumbly at a giant hole in the middle of the office.

It was M who eventually broke the silence.

"Was that what I think it was?" she asked.

"I think so," P answered quietly. "That was Waldo riding a giant earthworm."

M untied her wrists and tried to clean her glasses, which were completely covered in dust.

"That was Waldo?" she asked. "I thought it was a hairy little cowboy."

It Could Have Been Squirrels

My father and Rose Blackwood carefully walked around the giant hole in the room and picked up the treasure chest that had been left behind. We carried it outside only moments before the entire building collapsed, and was sucked into the large hole made by the earthworm.

I imagine that whoever visits that nameless island in the South Pacific will be shocked to find the crumbled remains of a criminal hideout there. As well as a giant worm, a clever monkey, and four very flattened villains.

We found the villains' horses hitched to a post behind their criminal hideout (or where their criminal hideout used to be), and we rode them back to the Baron Estate. Everyone was exhausted and starving from our long and difficult day, so as soon as we were home and washed up,

Rose and P cooked us all a special feast. As we ate, we stared at the treasure chest which was filled with more riches than we knew what to do with.

"I suppose it's all ours now. What should we do with it?" Rose asked. "Should we buy a bigger home? Better tools? A new horse? Sixteen new horses? Should we put it in the bank and save it?"

"Maybe we could all buy matching hats," P suggested.

"Why would we do that?" Rose asked.

"Look, I didn't question any of your stupid ideas," P retorted.

"I don't know," M said carefully. "It does feel rather strange having stolen treasure in the house. Perhaps we should try to find out who the treasure originally belonged to, and then return it to their families."

P and Rose stared at my mother as though she had suggested they take turns stuffing boiled potatoes up their nostrils. But I smiled. I looked back at the treasure and saw the three ghosts suddenly appear beside it. They were no longer dressed in scary ghost clothes or in the ridiculous bathing suits they had worn in the desert. The ghost who had been a baker was dressed as a baker. The ghost who had been a butcher was dressed as a butcher. The ghost who had been an accountant was dressed in a suit, and carried a little ghost briefcase filled with lots of boring ghost paperwork.

"I can already feel the curse beginning to break," the baker whispered excitedly. "We're going to be free."

"That's a great idea, M," I said. "I'm sure that if we go to the library, we can do some research and find out who Captain Affect stole all of this treasure from. We should return it to its owners. It's the right thing to do."

P and Rose grumbled for a bit about mansions and vacations and savings bonds and unusual hats, but, eventually, they agreed that it was the right thing to do. Finding the treasure was an adventure, but returning it to its rightful owners was what a real hero would do.

A quick trip to the library revealed that most of Captain Affect's stolen loot belonged to about a dozen different wealthy families in Europe, some of whom were actual royalty. After telling zorple-headed Aunt Dorcas that we were abandoning her for a few more weeks, we boarded our biggened Air Oh! Plane and flew to Europe with the treasure.

At first we had a bit of trouble getting into the castles to speak with some of the kings and queens who were the rightful owners of the treasure. Their guards didn't want to let us inside, even after we asked them nicely and complimented them on the strange hats they wore (P loved all of the royal guards' hats so much that he bought twenty of them to take home). But once the guards finally informed the royals that we wanted to give them priceless treasure, they happily invited us inside.

The first royal we visited lived in England. England was a wonderful country. In fact, it was probably my favorite country that we visited. Everyone was very kind and generous. In order to make us feel like we were at home, they all spoke nothing but English to us. Can you believe it? What a swell bunch of people. The Queen of England gladly accepted the golden crown and rubies and emeralds that Captain Affect had stolen from her ancestor, a woman by the name of Mary Stuart. I told her that there was a girl at my school who was also named Mary Stuart, but for some reason, the queen was not amused by that. Or by anything else, really . . .

A large part of the treasure was returned to the man who was king of both Sweden and Norway, who introduced himself simply as Oscar. Oscar and my father got along terrifically, even though neither could understand what the other was saying because King Oscar only spoke Swedish and Norwegian, and my father only spoke English and monkey. But they were able to communicate through hand gestures and grins, and through wiggling around the little fish that we were served for lunch. At the end of the visit they exchanged hats and promised to remain the closest of friends.

We continued across Europe to return stolen treasure to King Alfonso of Spain, King Christian of Denmark (whose giant mustache reminded me of my friend's father's mustache, which was actually two beaver tails glued to his face), Prince Albert of Monaco, as well as several other rich families that clearly didn't need the treasure, but, once they saw it, they swore they couldn't live without it.

The last of the treasure belonged to a rich woman who lived in Belgium. She had a mansion the size of a small city, with dozens of servants who were constantly bustling about. Some of them were actually paid to do nothing more than bustle, which they did with vigor. I suppose if you hire someone to bustle for you, you want them to bustle with vigor. What's the point of a vigorless bustler?

When we showed up at her mansion to present her with a bag full of gold coins (which my family could have used to buy everyone in the town of Pitchfork a new house and a steak dinner), she had yawned before tossing the bag to one of her servants, a skinny man with a skinny mustache, dressed in a skinny white tuxedo.

"Put this in the treasure room with the rest of my riches. Now go away. I think it's time for my second afternoon nap . . . or is this my third afternoon nap . . . I can't re . . ." she murmured before falling asleep on a giant satin pillow.

The servant took the bag of gold coins to a room that was large enough to fit fifty full grown elephants (or one hundred baby elephants. I suppose it depends on the sort of elephants you want to keep). After emptying the coins from the bag into his hands, he climbed a ladder and placed the money onto one of the many toweringly tall piles of golden coins, golden piles which reminded me of the hills of desert sand surrounding the Baron Estate. It was a very impressive room. In fact, if someone were to ask me to imagine all of the world's money, I would picture the contents of that room. There must have been millions of coins in there. Some of the piles were so tall that they appeared to be slowly swaying, ready to drop in an instant, creating an avalanche of gold that could literally drown you in riches.

"Wowwee!" I said loudly as I stared at all of the gold coins. "How many coins do you have here?"

The skinny servant quickly put his finger to his lips and shushed me from his place at the top of the ladder, letting me know that I would have to be quiet while I was in the treasure room. But then he answered my question, whispering to me while making hand gestures which were so elaborate, that at one point he accidentally tied his skinny fingers into a butterfly knot. He whispered a lot, going on and on and on, going into far more detail than I would have imagined possible for such a simple question.

Unfortunately, the servant spoke only in French. So even though he was able to answer my question (I'm guessing he did?), as well as several additional questions that I hadn't even asked (I'm assuming?), I was unable to understand any of his answers. But still, I wanted to be polite, so I acted appreciative anyway.

"Thank you," I whispered to him when he had finally finished. "I appreciate you talking so much. Please don't do it anymore though. It was very boring and confusing."

"*Je vous en prie*," he whispered back.

"*Gesundheit*," said my father. "Now, I think we should be going. We have a long trip back home, and I'm already quite sleepy. It's time, everybody. LET'S GO!"

The Belgian servant gasped. His eyes grew wide as he held his fingers up to his lips and hissed, begging us to stay quiet. And as P, M, Rose and I stepped out of the treasure room, I quickly realized why. The echo was quite powerful in that cavernous room, with the towering stacks of coins, and a little vibration had devastating effects.

There was a rumbling noise, and I turned back just in time to see the Belgian servant knocked off his ladder and drowned in a crashing wave of gold coins.

Poor guy.

Though I suppose it could have been worse.

It could have been squirrels.

THERE ARE SOME BENEFITS TO BEING A DUNCE

And now here I am, sitting in the corner of the schoolhouse, with a pointy dunce cap on my head while whispering my story to a mouse named Howard.

Howard was polite enough to listen the whole time, though I could tell from the expression on his face that he didn't believe a word of what I was saying. I suppose it is pretty unbelievable. I mean, there's no way that I would ever believe someone who told me that story. Unless they happened to have proof.

Which I have.

Let me explain.

There was one part of Captain Affect's treasure that we hadn't been able to return to its rightful owner.

The Wish Diamond.

James Reavis (the fake Vice President) was absolutely right when he told us that it was the most stolen diamond in the history of the world. We performed hours and hours of research, but we still couldn't figure out who its rightful owner was. We kept tracing the diamond back further and further in history. We followed it through the Renaissance, and the Dark Ages (which we learned were actually somewhat dimly lit because of the sparkles provided by the Wish Diamond), and even across the span of the Roman Empire. And it had been owned by people in every country in every continent in the world. It seemed as though the one thing uniting every person in history was that at one time, they had stolen the Wish Diamond.

"I'm baffled," M finally said as she dropped the oldest book in the library onto the table. "It says here that very little is known about the behavior of early cavemen, but we do know that one of their favorite games was stealing the Wish Diamond from each other."

"So are we supposed to find the first caveman or cave-woman and give them the diamond?" P asked.

"I don't think the first caveman or cavewoman would have much use for the diamond, Mr. Baron," Rose told him.

"Don't look now," M whispered. "But the librarian has just spotted the diamond. And I can tell by the greedy look in her eye that she's already planning on stealing it from us."

She was right. The sweet little old lady who had greeted us so kindly when we'd come into the library now looked as though she would gladly bash all of our brains in with her biggest book if it meant she had a chance to own that diamond. And it wasn't just the librarian. The Wish Diamond had caught every eye in the room. Nice, polite, friendly, and decent people suddenly had wickedness in their eyes as they stared at the shimmering diamond that would make them filthy rich. I saw several people slink outside and peer at us through the back window. I imagined that some of them were planning on following us home to the Baron Estate, where they would do whatever they could to take ownership of the most beautiful diamond in history, even if it meant separating our heads from our bodies.

My family huddled closely together and discussed what we should do next, when suddenly I felt a gentle tap on my shoulder. I ignored it at first, since I was distracted by thoughts of the Wish Diamond, but then I felt a very chilly and wet finger poke inside my ear.

"Augghhhh," I grimaced, turning around as I dried the inside of my ear. "Gross. Ghost spit."

The three ghosts smiled at me and waved. I noticed that each of them had a suitcase in his hand.

"Well, we're off," one of the ghosts said proudly.

"Yup," said another ghost. "The treasure has been returned, and Captain Affect's curse is now officially broken. We are finally free to move on to a better place."

"To Cleveland!" the third ghost said excitedly.

"Congratulations," I whispered. "But we haven't returned the last part of the treasure yet. We're still trying to find the rightful owner of the Wish Diamond. Do you have any idea who it is?"

The ghosts laughed.

"There is no original owner of the Wish Diamond. It's been stolen so many times that every person in the world can rightly say that they are the true owner of it. It belongs to everyone and to no one."

"So what should we do with it?" I asked.

The ghosts shrugged.

"We can't tell you that," said one of them. "But whatever you decide, please be careful. Hundreds of thousands of people have been killed for the Wish Diamond. It's bad luck, and it turns good people into evil people in a heartbeat. Anyway, thanks for your help, kid."

"I'm sorry to say that since the curse is now broken, you won't be turning into a ghost like us," another ghost said. "It's a shame. I think you would have been a pretty good one, W.B."

It was the nicest thing anyone had ever said to me. The ghosts all gave me a big, ghostly hug before they disappeared.

"What about you, W.B.?" Rose asked. "What do you think we should do with the Wish Diamond? Also, are you hugging your invisible friend? Because that's a little weird."

I thought for a moment, and then my brain did that funny thing it sometimes does in between being knocked around by my many trips, flips, falls, stumbles, bumbles, bumps, and thumps.

It had an idea.

"Hey, P?" I whispered. "May I please borrow your Shrinking Invention?"

Howard the mouse watched with a curious expression as I reached into my pocket and pulled out a very unique and very tiny item no larger than a peanut, though it was the most sparkly and stunning peanut that the world had ever seen.

It was actually the Wish Diamond, which I had shrunk.

I told my parents that if we were to keep the Wish Diamond for ourselves, we would have to spend the rest of our lives trying to protect it from greedy thieves. And what fun would that be? We could attempt to sell it, but I knew we wouldn't be able to. Why would anyone buy the diamond from us when they could save their money and just steal it from us instead? That's why no one had ever successfully sold the Wish Diamond before. It was too beautiful to be sold.

M handed me the diamond, and P handed me his Shrinking Invention. He had successfully adjusted the invention the previous day, so that it could shrink things to very specific sizes, which was necessary for me to carry out my plan.

"Of course we trust you, son," M said as she grinned. "After all, you're the one who risked his life to rescue that treasure from the bottom of the sea in the first place. You should decide what happens to the last part of it."

Rose Blackwood sighed as she nodded her head.

"I suppose that's fair," she said. "But next time we find a priceless treasure, can I be the one who decides what we do with it?"

With my parents and Rose shielding me from the prying eyes of the library patrons, I pressed the button at the end of the Shrinking Invention and shrunk the Wish Diamond to the size of a peanut. I hid it in my mouth.

When the librarian and the greedy crowd approached us as we were leaving, P told them that we no longer had the diamond, and if they needed proof, then they could search us.

Apparently, they needed proof. They grabbed us and turned us upside down, trying to shake the diamond out of us. They made us turn our pockets inside out. Rose emptied her handbag, and P emptied his cap. But of course, there was no diamond to be found.

"Where did you put it?" the librarian demanded, waving her fist in our faces. "We all saw that you had it in there! It was as big as a cannonball! Give it to me or I'll knock all of your teeth out! I'll rip your noses off and bury them in your backyard! I'll turn your skin inside out and cover you in salt!"

"We hid it," Rose told her with a wink, "somewhere in your library. First person to find it gets to keep it."

In a flash, the librarian and the rest of the crowd rushed back inside the library and began to tear it apart, shelf by shelf, wall by wall, in search of the diamond which was currently wedged behind my back teeth.

The next day, the whole town of Pitchfork gathered together to repair the torn-apart library. And as they rebuilt it, everyone kept a watchful eye on everyone else, just in case they happened to spot something that sparkled in the rubble.

I had brought the diamond to school so I could show

it to the class while I gave my report on what I'd done over my summer vacation. It was proof that everything I told them was the absolute truth.

Unfortunately, Miss Danielle was not interested in the truth, because the truth was too weird. The truth is often too weird when it comes to my family. So she made me sit in the corner and put on my dunce cap before I had the chance to show the little diamond to everyone. Which was a shame. I really wanted them all to have a chance to see it before I did what I did next.

"Here you go," I said to Howard, holding the shrunken Wish Diamond out to my little mouse friend. "Take it. It's yours."

Howard blinked twice as he turned his little mouse head to the side, uncertain if I was being serious or not. When he realized that I wasn't joking, Howard reached out and took the diamond before disappearing into his little hole in the wall. I imagined he was excited to show it to the other Howards, or maybe he was just going to stuff it into a little mouse closet for safekeeping. Either way, for the first time in history, the Wish Diamond had been given away instead of stolen. And that had to count for something, right?

Right?

Oh my goodness, did I just make a horrible mistake?

No. No, I didn't. I did the right thing.

. . . Didn't I?

I turned around to see what the rest of the class was doing and found that the classroom was empty. I looked at the clock on the wall and saw that school had ended almost an hour ago. I suppose Miss Danielle forgot to tell me. Or maybe she did tell me, but I was too busy whispering my story to Howard to pay attention.

I stood up and went to my desk, where I gathered all of my books and pencils and put them into my book bag. After stumbling over my chair and bonking my face against the wall, I gracefully made my way out of the classroom.

The sun was still shining brightly in the sky. It was Friday, which meant I'd have all day tomorrow and Sunday to join my parents in whatever their new adventure might be. P had recently invented something he called a Doppelgänger Device, and I was dying to know what it did. I didn't have a scientific brain, but I had recently discovered that I have a very curious brain, which wasn't too shabby a brain to have.

As I made my way down the schoolhouse stairs, preparing for my long walk across the Pitchfork Desert to the

Baron Estate, I spied something rather strange scuttling by. At first I wasn't quite certain what it was, but once my brain understood what my eyes were seeing, I realized that it was a squirrel carrying a diamond peanut. And since there is no such thing as a diamond peanut, I realized that it was actually the shrunken Wish Diamond that I had given to Howard the mouse.

I heard a thin, shrieking noise, and saw little Howard scampering down the schoolhouse steps, waving his angry little fist at the squirrel, which had clearly just stolen his diamond. He was followed by all of the other little Howards, who also waved their angry little mouse fists at the thief. The squirrel cackled happily as it made a mad dash for the nearest tree while staring at its new tiny treasure.

The squirrel (why is it always squirrels?) was staring at the diamond so intently, that it accidentally ran headfirst into the tree, knocking itself unconscious.

The Howards, seeing their chance to regain their treasure, hopped off the bottom step of the schoolhouse and scurried across the dirt towards the diamond. But when the Howards were two mouse-lengths away from the diamond, a little green lizard appeared out of nowhere and snatched the Wish Diamond up with its teeth.

The squirrel had regained consciousness, and he and

the Howards began to chase the lizard, which had already started to run towards the desert where it could enjoy its newly stolen prize.

But the lizard didn't have much time to enjoy it because suddenly a desert fox appeared from behind a bush. The fox ripped the diamond from the lizard's teeth before spinning around and preparing to run as fast as foxly possible in the other direction.

The fox had barely secured the diamond in her teeth before a large hawk came down from the sky and yanked it from the fox's mouth with its large claws. The hawk flapped its powerful wings and took off, leaving the fox, the lizard, the squirrel, and the Howards staring longingly up at the little diamond that they had each owned for a precious moment.

Shortly after the hawk had returned to its place high in the sky, I spotted a large cluster of crows, vultures, ducks, geese, owls, parrots, and sparrows, which had all stopped midair and changed direction when they spotted their fellow flyer's newfound treasure. The birds began to chase the hawk across the sky, each one crying and croaking and cawing and shrieking and screeching and chirping for that shiny little peanut which they believed was rightfully theirs.

I suppose the animals are all still chasing one another, fighting over ownership of that silly little diamond. It might have been wrong for me to introduce that kind of greed into the animal kingdom. Then again, it was probably very, very, very wrong for my family to introduce a stick wielding monkey that rides throughout the world on a giant earthworm. But to be honest, I had more important things on my mind, like my father's new invention . . . and the banana cream pie that I knew we had in the ice box. In fact, my mind was *especially* focused on the banana cream pie that I knew we had in the ice box. I love banana cream pie.

While my mind was distracted with thoughts of adventures and pie, I accidentally stumbled over a twig in the middle of the path, flipped end over end, and landed right on top of my head. But for some reason, the fall didn't hurt, even though I had landed directly onto a pile of rocks.

I realized that I was still wearing the pointy dunce cap that Miss Danielle had put on my head as punishment for lying. It hadn't taught me a lesson like my teacher intended, but it did protect my skull from what would have otherwise been a very painful fall.

So I suppose there are some benefits to being a dunce.

EXTRAVAGANT ADJECTIVES

Eric Bower is a large, furry-faced man, who is married to a lovely, curly-haired woman named Laura. They live in a one-hundred-year old cottage in sunny Southern California, with their fuzzy and willfully difficult cat and dictator, Freyja. Eric enjoys writing silly books, playing his acoustic guitar, and using an extravagant number of unnecessary adjectives.

Bringing Words to Life

Agnieszka Grochalska lives in Warsaw, Poland. She received her MFA in Graphic Arts in 2014. Along the way, she explored traditional painting, printmaking, and sculpting, but eventually dedicated her keen eye and steady hand to drawing precise, detailed art reminiscent of classical storybook illustrations. Her current work is predominantly in digital medium, and has been featured in group exhibitions both in Poland and abroad.

She enjoys travel and cultural exchanges with people from around the world, blending those experiences with the Slavic folklore of her homeland in her works. When she isn't drawing or traveling, you can find her exploring the worlds of fiction in books and story-driven games.

Agnieszka's portfolio can be found at agroshka.com.